WHEN LOVE BLOSSOMS

BOOK 2 OF THE KINDRED LAKE SERIES

ELAINE STOCK

G†G
Publishing

When Love Blossoms by Elaine Stock

Published by GTG Publishing

ISBN: 978-0-9995763-4-2 Trade Paperback

You can receive Elaine Stock's novella, *And You Came Along* for Free! This story is a prequel to the Kindred Lake Series, though it can be read by itself. Please click onto: https://elainestock.com/free-gift-for-you

Dedication:

To my husband, Wally, and my father, Charles, in gratitude for showing me what love is all about. It's a scary world out there and I'm thankful you're there for me.

*K*ierra Madden grasped the phone tighter in both disbelief and gratitude. "You'd like to book a room for an uncertain time period, Mr. Delaney?"

"Well, yes, but not if you're so formal. It's Ryan. Got that?"

She straightened her posture and squared back her shoulders, not that *Ryan* could see her. Reservations for Kindred Lake Inn were down compared to the previous year. A glance at her register showed not one booking until the first weekend of June. Shaky finances might sorely impact her family moving in with her that very mid-April day. She would benefit from Delaney's stay, and brushed off her slight irritation of his straightforwardness and assertion. He did have a rich voice and a soft twang. Perhaps he was pleasant, after all.

About to tell him he was welcome to stay as long as he liked, a gnat-annoying eeep eeep of a U-Haul truck backing up sailed through the kitchen window, cracked open an inch to let in a breath of fresh air and hope. Her mother, sister and niece had arrived.

"Are you there?" Ryan said.

Kierra reined back her focus to the caller. As her new guest

Delaney had the potential to save the day, financially speaking. She patted her right pocket, its emptiness a reminder of her weakening circumstances.

"Yes, Mr. De...sorry, Ryan. I'm here." She glanced out the window again just as the truck backed over one of her Garden-Club-prized red rose bushes, not that colorful blossoms graced her property this time of year in Pennsylvania, when spring warmth seemed an eternity away. She spun from the disaster erupting outside the inn. This place of business had become a true solace from the crazies of life and she hoped it remained that way. "I'll be delighted to see you whenever you arrive. The room's yours as long as you'd like. I look forward to meeting you." She disconnected after their goodbyes and sprinted outdoors. Her life was about to change. Again.

Determined to make her family's acceptance to move in with her work, she clamped down on her resolution to provide a needed refuge for her mom, sister, and niece. Not one of them had a halfway decent alternative. One way or the other, they'd have a happy ending. Family first. No matter the past years of shaky ties, right?

Of course, family first. That was her new mantra and she was sticking to it.

Zoe, her thirteen-year-old niece, stood on the passenger side of the U-Haul. Dressed in black Capri pants with a black shirt, the girl wrapped her pale arms around her middle. To ward off the chill in the air? To cover up her dreary outfit? At least the dark color matched her natural ebony hair that hung halfway down her back. Uncertain whether Zoe had received an ounce of TLC from anyone today, Kierra smiled warmly.

The driver emerged from the truck. His sweat-soaked gray T-shirt clung to his torso. As he stretched his tattooed-sleeved arms and rolled his shoulders, his untied greasy hair swayed from side to side. This grubby, grimy man had sat beside her niece during the entirety of the trip? Her mom was the one who needed to be by the girl's side. And where was her sister?

A car horn blasted with the fervor of someone who loved making an entrance.

Ah, Tessa had arrived.

Tessa, in her cosmetically challenged, once silver two-door Ford Focus, pulled behind the truck. She exploded from behind the wheel. The pink and purple gauzy-cotton outfit she'd slid her willowy body into resembled the *I Dream of Jeannie* garments their favorite TV sitcom actress often wore—the few times Kierra and Tessa watched the old comedy station together and shared laughter. The loud cannonball-color suited her sister's fiery temperament, which Kierra hoped her sis left behind in Boston.

Tessa waved. "Hey, sis. We're home."

Kindred Lake Inn was definitely not Tessa's home. Her sister, niece and mother could find temporary refuge here, but not a permanent home. They'd have to straighten out that fact later after everyone settled in.

Guilt stabbed at her insides and she flinched. What happened to *family first*?

A second stranger climbed out the truck. There had been two men seated besides Zoe? A tad better dresser, he wore jeans, a clean T-shirt touting a rock band, and a Red Sox cap over carrot-red clipped hair. He also stretched, arms high in the air. "That was one insane long road trip." He flashed Tessa a grin. "But I'll do anything for you."

Tessa reached for his arms and wrapped them around her middle. "Oh, how I know, Sam. Wish you were moving in with me."

Forgotten Zoe, lithe from spending hours on the gymnastics floor, but having an unbendable heart and spirit, stood expressionless as her mom then hugged the tattoo-dude. Kierra rushed to the assorted foursome, her heart skipping a beat for her niece. She too was a forgotten daughter.

With one sweep of her arms Kierra tucked Zoe in a tight hold.

"Hey, Aunt Kierra." Zoe squirmed and backed away a good foot. "Love you, but I'm no kid anymore. I'm fine."

"You're always the little girl I've never had."

Zoe blushed. "Aw."

"Sis," Tessa said, loud enough for all to hear. "It's not exactly too late for you in the kid department."

The two guys nodded. Total strangers to her, she wished for the superpower of disappearing into the ether and away from the judgmental scrutiny of others.

Kierra pasted a halfhearted smile on her lips and chose to ignore her sister's taunt. *Family first.* "I'm happy to see you, Zoe. I'm glad it worked out that you're moving in during school break."

"It would have been easier to wait until the start of a new school year."

"Well, kiddo," Tessa said. "Our leaving couldn't wait a day longer."

For her niece's sake, Kierra wanted to switch the focus off of her. "Hi, sis. Where's Mom?"

Tessa lifted her chin toward the car. "Back seat. Sound asleep. She nearly had a fit when we wouldn't drop her off five miles ago to get in her extra steps for the day then dozed off as if she popped a sleep remedy."

Mom and her exercise. At least Anna was devoted to a cause outside of micromanaging her two grown daughters' lives. "She zonked out that fast?"

Tessa shrugged. "I'm not complaining, especially after she served crabby on toast this morning for breakfast before we left."

Zoe tugged Kierra's hand. "I would have sat with Grandma, but tons of boxes and other junk made it impossible. I chose the truck."

"Chose, Zoe?" A sour look crossed Tessa's face. "Try issuing an ultimatum like you're riding in the truck or tough luck." She glanced at Kierra. "Actually, sis, I take back what I said a few seconds ago. You're the lucky one, without kids. Like kittens and puppies, they're cute until they become older."

Lucky? Sadness encased Kierra from head to toe. If she had to pin a color to the feeling she'd liken it to gray, like a lifetime of rainy days without a glimpse of sunlight. And she not only hurt for herself, but for her niece as well. She feared if she cautioned her sister to think twice before she spoke that her advice would be a waste of effort.

Zoe's lips stretched in an obvious fake smile. "Thanks for the mommy-love, Mom."

Kierra bent to whisper in her niece's ear. "Honey, I'm sure you would have sat with Grandma, if given a chance. You're a caring soul."

Zoe's chin dipped. "I wasn't exaggerating about any room in the car."

"I believe you."

"Awesome. Someone does."

Kierra tousled her niece's thick hair then glanced at Tessa. How could they have the same parents, the same five-foot-five slim build, and share countless likes and dislikes, and yet behave in totally different ways that a stranger might have difficulty linking them as sisters? "This bail-out is only for a couple of months until you get back on your feet."

Tessa snorted, a familiar sign of pure frustration. "You try getting kicked out by your landlord, with a mother and daughter in tow. Tell me what to do with fifteen years of accumulated garbage? And Mom? You know she can't cope squat with changes."

Kierra could quip about her own woes, but held back. Her sister had enough of a headache to deal with and didn't need to hear her version of a pity-party. "Sorry."

Tessa narrowed her eyes, reminding Kierra of their mother.

"You don't know half of what it's like dealing with a messy life, not the way you're conveniently stuck in this town."

Stuck? After years of extensive hotel management and savings, she'd struck out on her own and purchased the brick Queen Anne house in the town of Kindred Lake and until recently made a decent living opening it to guests as a bed and breakfast inn. Since she was the innkeeper, as well as the cook, the chambermaid, and chief garbage-take-outer, it was a must to be tied to the inn, the place whose doors she'd opened for Tessa. But, her sister needed love and support, not disdain.

"Girls," her mom called from beside Tessa's car.

Oh, boy. Here it comes. Kierra glanced right. When had she stepped beside her sister?

Anna stood straight, her perfect posture seemingly adding inches to her five-foot-two height. Dressed in pale lavender sweats, she appeared more the athlete than the consummate and award-winning food blogger that she was. She crossed her arms.

"I adapt fine enough to change. That's why I came here, in hope of a new beginning." Anna paused as she swiped a hard look over both Kierra and Tessa. "But now? I'm doubtful this is the right place for me. Crabby on toast...if that wasn't such a delicious food pun for me to use on my blog, believe me, you two would never hear the end of it."

"We will never hear the end," Tessa mumbled.

Kierra ribbed her in the side with her always-ready elbow.

"Phooey." Anna waved at the air. "Good to see you, Kierra."

Mom, just open your arms and I'll come running to give you a hug.

Unsure of what to do with her own arms, Kierra stuffed her hands into her pockets. "I'm glad you accepted my invitation."

Anna glanced at the inn and shook her head. "What other choice did I have?"

Did that make Kierra's offer for her family to move in with her the first desirous choice or a second one, more like a settlement that would have to do?

"There's a comfy room waiting for you, one with bright colors, plants, and lots of sunshine." Kierra gestured toward the front entrance. "Come on in and I'll show you the changes since your last visit. My place is your place."

Her mom didn't budge. "Yes, it's your dwelling, all right."

That familiar knot Kierra hadn't experienced in a while pinched in her neck. Her need to please her mother always backfired. "How does a cool drink sound, Mom? The long drive from Massachusetts must have you thirsty."

"We stopped along the way for drinks. In Jersey. Zoe enjoyed a soft serve ice cream cone while I enjoyed non-sweetened iced coffee and the others guzzled cola." She wrinkled her nose. "I tried to convince them that sugar only serves to destroy their insides, but no one listened. No one ever does."

The commotion from the men unloading furniture from the U-Haul lured Tessa away. Zoe shuffled over to the shade of a tall pine tree and sat cross-legged on the grass. A shade of awful sadness drained the teen's face of color. With divorced parents, a standoffish grandmother, plus today's move from her hometown, the girl's troubles must have pressed with elephant-like weight on her small shoulders.

Kierra continued with the subject of more importance, her niece's comfort. "I think it's best to get Zoe indoors. Want to join me?"

"You always know what's best." If another woman had muttered those words, Kierra would interpret them as praise. Coming from her mother, she knew better.

"I'll help Zoe settle inside. If you'd rather stay outdoors that's fine with me."

Anna's brow lifted. "The word settle does sound appealing."

Surprised when a smile overtook her mom, softening her features, Kierra motioned for Zoe to join them. Her niece stood and reached for her grandmother's arm. Side by side they walked at a good clip toward the proudly standing 1880s former stately house with black shutters, its freshly painted white porch with a wrap-around veranda on the right side, and its original, intact slate roof. Under Kierra's hard-working hands, the place had become the town of Kindred Lake's gem of a bread and breakfast inn.

Well, technically, the only B&B in town. As for gem, she hoped that lovely term wouldn't varnish like the clientele had as of late. She hoped the lure of Kindred Lake sitting pretty behind the inn would beckon them back. She certainly hoped for a lot these days.

Kierra caught up with her mom and niece just short of the brick steps.

"Zoe, there's a place"—Anna pointed to the veranda—"for the two of us to enjoy each other's company and chitchat."

Although her mom and niece continued indoors, Kierra stopped. Had her ears betrayed her or had she heard correctly her mom wish for time with her grandchild rather than her food blog and its umpteen devoted viewers? With a boost in spirit, she dashed indoors.

"This place always deceives me," Anna said as soon as Kierra shut the double doors behind her. She ran a finger on a table's marble surface, likely checking for dust that she wouldn't find. "It looks much bigger from the outside. Is there definitely room for us, especially if you have guests checking in?"

"Not a worry. Believe me, based on the hours I put into cleaning this place, I can say without exaggeration it's pretty spacious. There are seven comfortable-sized bedrooms upstairs. For your privacy, I converted the downstairs office to another guest room where you will stay. It's nice and big. Zoe and Tessa will share a room upstairs." She thought about the one guest, not plural. She hoped her mom didn't dwell upon the availability of rooms due to a lack of business; she was trying not to sink further into the blues. "A guest will arrive later this afternoon. And with my apartment over the old carriage house, we'll all have our privacy."

"Is that another way of saying we won't be tripping over each other, as in intruding in one's personal space?"

Nope. She wasn't going to play the game of semantics with her mother. "Guests can easily check in and enjoy their stay."

Anna furrowed her brows. "I'll like to go to my room."

Kierra gestured in the other direction toward the kitchen. "Would you like a drink? A sandwich?"

"I'm not hungry. Show me my room."

"I'll find it with you." Zoe grasped her grandma's hand. "This place is way cool to explore."

"Mom," Kierra called as her niece and mother made their way down the hall. "Sorry about the ratty yellow bedspread and curtains. I redid the room but never got around to those extras."

"No problem."

Zoe glanced over her shoulder. "If mine is nicer, I'll swap bedspreads, Aunt Kierra. As Grandma says, no problem."

"That's very nice of you to do," Kierra said in an upbeat tone. She hoped her family could remain problem-free.

A metallic crash launched Kierra outside again. Along with flattened prized roses, she now owned a trashed trashcan. Its contents spewed on the white stone driveway like wilted flowers.

Tessa rubbed at a sheepish grin. "Oops. We needed to back the truck closer to the house. I'll clean up the mess. Why do you keep the trash can there anyways?"

Kierra would only waste her breath if she explained that today was trash-collection day and bit down on her bottom lip. She needed to get away from Tessa before she passed the point of regret. She fished into her khaki slacks and withdrew two sets of house keys then shoved both into her sister's hand.

"Mom's in her room. I suspect Zoe may want lunch. The fridge is loaded. Help yourself, though I expect you to help fill it for the remainder of your stay. I have a consultation for a wedding that will be held here. Call my cell if there's an emergency, but I won't be long. An hour at the most. I'll be back before my guest is due to check in."

Tessa clucked. "Just like that? Poof, and you're gone?" She cast lazy, lingering eyes at her two pals flanking her. A warm smile raised her lips bright with fresh candy apple lipstick. "I haven't introduced you to my friends."

"Another time, Tessa."

"Fine. Leave. What else is new?"

"Oh, Tessa—"

"Don't oh-Tessa me. I shouldn't expect you to put your family first."

"I'm not exactly putting you guys last." She turned from her sister and her two pals and started toward her car.

Tessa squawked. "What did I tell you? No one cares."

"I care about you, Tessa, honey," one of the guys said.

Behind the Subaru's wheel she turned over the engine and started to pull out of the driveway. A bicyclist on a serious looking black-framed bike with white stripes in its center screeched to a halt within inches of her vehicle. Unsure of whether to be alarmed or intrigued, she slid from her car.

The rider dismounted his bike. Tall and toned, in need of a shave, he stood in the posture of confidence. His chocolate brown eyes stole her breath. She counted on that shade of brown, as well as the rest of him, to materialize in her dreams later that evening. Was he lost? She could certainly give him directions...to a place... or to someone. Kindred Lake was a small town; she knew just about everyone. She snickered to herself. He surely wasn't looking for her. With his looks, that was a shame, indeed.

Unable to move, and not wanting to, she stared at the unsmiling feast before her eyes. She reminded herself that she wasn't interested in the whole romance scene. She was over that.

"Ryan Delaney," he said. His voice brought to her mind a

Beethoven cello sonata she'd heard on the radio the other day, strong and resonant. "Are you Ms. Madden?"

Like a stunned animal, she remained fixed in place. With the English language vanished suddenly from her brain, she ogled the black spandex bicycle shorts, a navy blue jersey, and a yellow windbreaker outlining a fine selection of solid male muscle.

"I'm early, but if my room isn't ready, I'll come back later."

Oh, her guest. Ryan-Got-That. The Room 3 reservation.

She hooked a finger under the collar of her apricot colored blouse—the shade she hoped wasn't creeping across her cheeks—and stretched the fabric from her neck. "Yes, to your first question." She extended a hand to shake. "Please, call me Kierra. You biked from Maryland?"

"I did." He checked his watch. "I can come back in a few hours if the room isn't ready."

"No. Stay." She felt like an actress in a low-budget B movie. A very bad one.

Stay, he did. Silent, watchful of every movement she made.

"You're in Room 3. The Royal Room. It has a private bath."

He tilted his head. "Good. I expected one."

"It's upstairs, third room to the left. The door's unlocked. I'll show you if you'd like."

"Thanks, but I'll find it."

"You can leave your bike on the far side of the driveway, opposite of where my sister and her two helpers are unloading the U-Haul. Don't worry though. My family's moving in won't dampen your privacy or quiet."

He scanned the grounds. "Believe me, this is bucolic compared to the city life I'm accustomed to in Baltimore. As for family, unless they strum bass guitar two in the morning, I'm fine."

Oh, he was surely fine.

"That makes two of us." She eyed his bike. "Your...uh...possessions?" What did one use to carry clothes on a bike trip across various states?

He patted his shoulder. Talk about delayed reactions. She hadn't noticed his knapsack until then.

"I travel light."

"Oh."

What great stimulating conversation she provided. She could hear future guests gush.

"Kindred Lake Inn? That's a fine place. Don't expect intelligent conversation from the innkeeper, though. She's a bit addled in the head."

With his fast-paced stride to the location where he could park his bike, it was apparent Delaney couldn't care less about what she had to say.

He paused halfway. "If anyone should phone the inn's main number, I'm to receive no calls except from my daughter, Bella."

Before she could reassure him that he wouldn't be disturbed, Zoe rushed out the door, zipped down the drive, and nearly barged into the new guest.

"Come quickly. Mom just walked in on Grandma and a whole new world war is beginning."

Without wasting precious seconds to reply, she bounded the steps. She'd check up on Delaney...Ryan...whichever name he preferred, later.

2
_____

*R*yan liked what he saw. The room, his new home for an unknown while, was nicer than what he expected. A gold crisscross wallpaper pattern accented with red and soft gold curtains framed a nice-sized—probably a queen—mahogany antique bed canopied with the same curtain material. Plump matching red armchairs, both with hassocks, flanked a large bow window, perfect for reading especially since no way would he watch television with its likelihood of the news mirroring his nightmares. He could see why his hostess called Room 3 *The Royal Room*.

His hostess, huh? Yep, Ms. Madden...Kierra...regrettably snagged his attention with her unusual combo of hot-looking dark brownish hair, bright spring green eyes, and a curvy waist, but also with a wholesome and kind smile, which he found rare these days. He rubbed his temples. Women...work...wandering.

In need of getting his mind off of the pressures riding his shoulders, he glanced about the room, taking in the Persian blue and red rugs scattered over the honey shade of the maple flooring. An old-fashioned armoire stood proudly opposite the bed but, situated next to a closet with its door painted the subdued gold trim of the room, he assumed the cabinet hid a television and extra blankets and pillows. He'd check it out later, but between visiting with his daughter, reading books stashed on his Kindle reader, and zipping about on his bike exploring the town and the hills surrounding Kindred Lake, he'd keep plenty busy.

When he'd made his decision to hop on his bike and pedal north, his friend Zander and his wife of two years, Jacey, invited Ryan into their home for a few days visit. They lived an hour south of Kindred Lake, closer to the Maryland border. Between their friendship and location, he couldn't resist. Caleb, Jacey's son from her first marriage, a bundle of high-test energy and fun, was smart and cute as anything. Ryan hoped they would soon add a new addition to their family. A baby girl to dress in frilly dresses or a little boy to build tree houses with. Caleb already intimated he wanted a brother. Yep, lucky Zander. He was happy for Z. He deserved a good dosage of joy after what he'd gone through.

Ryan shrugged off his reminiscing and shucked off the knapsack from his back and onto the bed. In three steps he stood before the large window. The lake spread out before two prominent rolling hills. He'd definitely have to search for hiking trails or blaze his own. Lately, life solo style was his hearty chunk of contentment. He was a free person, relatively speaking, and he was thankful about it.

"I'm not leaving Grandma," a high-pitched shout came from downstairs.

"Listen to me, Zoe. Let me and Kierra handle this."

"Handle?" came a mature, scratchy voice. "I'm no rubbish to handle and cart to the road like garbage."

Must be Kierra's clan.

Ryan faced the door to the hallway. He could leave right then, not concerned about forfeiting one night's stay already pre-paid. Although his muscles could use a rest, he could mount his bike and pedal away to the next destination, wherever that might be. Not like he needed a roof over his head or an assured breakfast to start his day off on a supposed right note. Look at the mess that reliance had gotten him into the past few years. However, if he took off he'd defeat his sole purpose for arriving in town: to visit with Bella.

Both weary and wary, he decided to stay put in hope the commotion passed and that it was a one-time nuisance. As long as he had peaceful nights he wouldn't complain. It wasn't as if he planned to hang around the place 24/7.

"You're awful," came another shout.

Footfall pounded up the stairs followed by a jog past his room. He suspected it was the teen girl that he almost collided with after he'd secured his bike. For a slightly built girl, her weight rattled the door. A key jingling followed by a door slam undid the rest of his nerves. His sigh was snipped when her sobs leaked through the thin walls. No stranger to teen angst, he flung his door open and approached the room next to his.

He rapped his knuckles lightly on the shut door. When the only reply was a fresh burst of sobs he tried again, but this time a bit stronger.

"Mom? Aunt Kierra? Go away. Leave me alone."

"No, it's me." He realized she had no idea who he was and likely didn't care. "I'm Ryan, from the room next door."

"What?" She half choked, half snorted. "Are you going to tell me to keep it down?"

"No way. I'm sorry you're hurting. Hey—I get where you're coming from."

"How? We don't know each other."

His fifteen-year-old daughter often flung that same cold truth his way. "I care, that's all. I don't like to see anyone upset."

"I don't want to talk."

"Do you mean this very second or forever and ever?"

A groan lashed back at him. "I mean never, like go away and play shrink elsewhere."

"Do you like to take walks?" He was thinking of Bella, of how once upon a time she used to join him on long walks through the woods behind his home when she came to visit on weekends. Of the times he'd get her to speak about the things troubling her, that inevitably led them to share bad jokes that always made them laugh. "I have two large ears that make for great listening." He had to lighten this poor girl's mood. "They're quite impressive, these Dumbo-sized ears. They're large but come in handy for times like now."

"Dumbo? Like the elephant in the cartoon?"

"Exactly." He leaned against the door relieved she sounded calmer.

"How old are you?" she asked. "You're not like grandpa age?"

He held back a chuckle. "I'm ancient. Try thirty-four."

"That's Aunt Kierra's age. My mom's two years older than both you and my aunt. That's why she doesn't understand me."

He wasn't about to argue with a teenager that a thirty-six-year-old mom wouldn't fail to understand her child because of her advanced age. He tried shifting the conversation back to the girl's needs. "Well, I understand you...hey, what's your name."

"Zoe."

"Zoe, I can't blame you for being frazzled. You're in a new place and everyone else is likely upset and short in patience. These changes are pretty scary, huh?"

"You got that straight."

He hated talking through barriers. "Want to open the door a little? I'm not a monster."

Zoe laughed.

He smiled. He'd actually got the girl to laugh, how about that? Maybe he'd eventually get her serious aunt to smile as well. Kierra, as beautiful as she was, could stand to chuckle once or twice.

The door opened. An inch. That was a start.

A pair of blue eyes peered at him.

"You're thirty-four? You look younger for someone that old."

He pulled at his chin. "Daily exercising helps."

"Like you work out at the gym?"

"Only in the winter. Otherwise, it's a lot of bicycle riding."

"I should have guessed that, based on your biking clothes." The door yawned open another inch. "What do you do, Ryan?"

"I chase bad guys."

Her brows lifted. "You're a cop?"

"A reporter." That was tamping it down a bit, but he didn't need Zoe to crush on him if she learned that he was a Baltimore news anchor, regardless of his extended leave of absence status.

"So, you're no shrink?"

He draped a look of self-pity across his face and sighed. "Guess not. No fancy certificates collect dust on my office walls."

She giggled. "You're cool, anyways." She looked away then back. "It's just that this change is new to me. I think Mom and Grandma are also freaking. You know, it's tough lately."

"I hear you, and I'm sorry it's been rough for you. I'm glad you're feeling a tad better. Say when if you'd enjoy a walk and talk time. Your mom is welcome to come along."

"Do we have to ask Mom? She's into healthy stuff, but we kind of dig our own space if you know what I mean. Aunt Kierra is a whole different story. She likes hiking and stuff."

Yep, her aunt's slim attractive body spoke volumes of someone that treasured the outdoors, as well as plain good old hard work. Somehow though, he couldn't quite envision the innkeeper in question as accompanying him on a stroll around Kindred Lake.

"Ryan, I'm going to chill for a few minutes then help Mom unpack. We got kicked out of our place and we're staying put here for a while. But, it's all good, right?"

"It will work out for the best." He flashed her a sincere, warm smile. "Take it easy."

"Sorry about the noise."

"No worries. I'll see you around."

"You bet."

He waited until the girl closed the door, this time gently. He pivoted to head back to his own room and nearly jumped back against the door. Kierra stood inches away.

3

"Thank you, Ryan, for what you said to Zoe. I appreciate you calming her down." Kierra motioned for them to walk toward the stairs, away from her niece's room and possibly listening ears.

"No problem." He sat down on the top step. "Sit with me a second or two."

She did, leaving only inches separating them. The thing was, she wanted to join him, suddenly unconcerned if the time spanned seconds or hours. "I'm worried about Zoe."

"Did you hear the whole conversation I had with her?"

"Yes, including the Dumbo part. Very cute, by the way. I was downstairs with my mom and sister when Zoe fled the room. I left as soon as I could to check on her." She looked into his brown eyes. Earlier when they'd first met his eye color had her thinking of chocolate. This close though, rich variations of mahogany and chestnut came to mind. "This is a major relocation, let alone upheaval for them. Mom moved in with Tessa and her husband after Zoe was born...but after years of bickering Dan tilted their world by leaving them following up with divorce papers. Tessa has been on the slow rebound, but when she became recently unemployed when the factory relocated overseas, everything else seemed to fall apart. Her landlord raised the rent and when she couldn't pay it, he couldn't wave bye-bye fast enough." She paused, wondering if Ryan cared about these details about her family. She imagined he had his own list of issues. He might have saddled his bike and pedaled mile after mile for several good reasons.

"Do you think Tessa's landlord raised the rent purposely to get her out? Sadly, it happens often." Concern etched his voice. "That same trouble happened to my friends. Actually, the lack of a place to live had brought them together when they got stuck in the middle of a blizzard. Deep in love, they married not long after they met, on New Year's Day."

She gasped and covered her mouth.

He squinted at her. "If they were anther couple I'd narrow it down to impulsiveness, but not with—"

"Jacey and Zander," she said, confident she had the right couple in mind. Not many folks she knew could claim their special story. "A beautiful couple who were meant to meet."

His mouth gaped open.

"Don't be surprised. Jacey's one of my dearest friends." She grinned wide. "Kindred Lake's a typical small town. Everyone knows each other, if not personally than at least by sight."

"Right, you are. Let me remove the smirk of amazement off my face." He rubbed hard at his mouth.

She cracked a laugh.

He pointed a finger at her. "You have a pretty smile when you laugh."

"Do I? I haven't heard that compliment much." She began ticking off on her fingers in an exaggerated flair. "Let's see...there was that one guy...oh, wait. He was talking to his reflection in the store mirror. There was the other... Nah. That was the little boy chatting with his grandma. Hmm. There was—"

He snatched her fingers in midair. "Oh, stop."

She leaned back against the step. "How do you know Jacey and Zander?"

"Zander is one cool pal. I knew him when he was a detective."

"Were you a cop?"

"No."

She waited for more. If she gave him plenty of breathing room, he'd likely share about himself.

He averted his eyes and remained quiet.

"Oh, wait. Both you and Zander are from Baltimore. You've been pals forever and then some?"

"Yes, we've know each other since the age of four. One of these days I'll get a T-shirt made touting Baltimore Born, Raised, and Happy."

He didn't appear that happy. Funny, she wanted to make him happy.

"Did you know Jacey before she met Zander?" she asked.

"No. Zander introduced us. I was Z's best man at their wedding."

"I wish I could have gone. I'd confirmed the invitation but came down with the flu."

"Sorry to hear that. To think we might have met then."

"I saw the wedding album, but I don't recall seeing you."

He pulled at his chin. "I shaved my beard off after the wedding."

An image of a gentleman in a black suit, handsome but sporting a thick beard and mustache flashed before her. She usually didn't care for beards, but on him it looked good. Actually, hot-looking. "Oh, yes. Right. I think I do remember seeing a photo of you with a glass of champagne lifted in a toast."

He nodded. "Yes, that would be me. How did you and Jacey meet?"

His abrupt deflection away from himself didn't escape her notice.

"There's a great diner in town. Ha, the only diner in town. Rick's Diner."

His shoulders relaxed; his fisted hands unfurled. "Yes, I've seen the place often, but never ate there."

"Oh? Have you lived in Kindred Lake?"

"No, but have visited...but not enough. My daughter lives with her mom outside of town." After a pause, he said, "That's a whole different story. You were saying...?"

"Jacey waited on tables there. She was awesome—loved by everyone. Sadly, her story is similar to my sister's. As I'm sure you know, a few days before Christmas Jacey's landlord served her an eviction's notice. Then to compound matters, her boss also fired her because she showed up late one day for work. She left town with her four-year-old son in toll." In need of a hug from the sad memories of her friend's departure, Kierra wrapped her arms around her middle. "My one true friend in Kindred Lake left."

Ryan inched closer. Her breath hitched.

"I know the feeling. I was sorry to see Zander leave. We hung out together a lot. At least they're not far from here."

She nodded. "You're right, but now that they're married I've been trying to give them some privacy."

"I hear you, but I just visited with them before coming here. I think they'd enjoy your company." A tiny spark lit his eyes. "I can't stop thinking about how they drove smack into a blizzard close to the Maryland border. Zander was heading north and—"

"Jacey south."

"And they collided. Literally. Praise God no one was hurt."

Ah, he was a believer. "Yes, thank God."

"A sweet couple offered them their cabin." He smiled. "They fell in love, married, and live in the cabin they've expanded into home sweet home."

She sighed dreamily. "A fairytale come true."

"I'd say, especially since Zander's father was actually Jacey's landlord, the one that kicked her out."

"Happy endings do occur when least expected. This June, the Kindred Lake Inn will host a special wedding that is proof positive to the theory of hope and love."

Ryan lifted a brow.

"My friend, Cami, is marrying an old schoolmate, Gavin. Would you believe Cami—along with a host of other kids—used to bully Gavin and his family?"

"That's taking kiss and make up literally. Must be a Kindred Lake specialty, this love business."

Love, as in romantic love? With someone who loved reciprocally back with his whole heart? Someone who respected her for the individual she was...without hiding secrets? She wouldn't know. She bounced onto her feet. "Speaking of, I have to run. I have an appointment to meet with those two."

Ryan stood. "I enjoyed our chat."

"Me too. Here's a confession: I'm rusty when it comes to social chitchat."

"I failed to notice."

The left side of her mouth lifted reflexively in surprise. "I'm glad."

He scrubbed his face with a hand. "I'm beat. Guess the trip here is finally catching up with me."

"After biking those miles, I'd be exhausted too."

Grunts gushed through the open front door. Like a cold wind, the sound changed the warm atmosphere and mood.

"I can't hold this much longer," one of Tessa's helpers said.

"Hold it, pal. Don't let—"

A crash came followed by a whistle of profanity.

"I told you."

"You think you broke it?"

"Me break it? You were on the other end."

Kierra winced. "That didn't sound good."

"You gotta be kidding," Tessa shouted. "That's Mom's teapot

collection. She'll dice me in pieces and sauté me, or worse, she'll lecture me for eternity."

Ryan gripped the banister.

"Where you going?" Kierra said.

He flashed a grin, as if to say it wasn't necessary to ask. "To help."

"But you're tired. You haven't had a chance to change and relax. Thanks, but no thanks. You're the guest, Ryan. Take it easy."

Another crash came from below.

"Right. I don't think that's possible until those two bozos are gone, your inn remains intact, and your sister is happy."

Before she could tell him that seemed unrealistic, at least the happy-sister part, he trotted downstairs.

"Hey, want a hand or two?" Ryan asked as he approached Tessa's companions.

"Cool," the two guys chorused with relief stamped across their faces.

She watched as Ryan coordinated the chaos and turned it into smooth order. The three men managed to move the rest of the boxes and assorted other items from the truck into her family's new guest rooms. Tessa pointed out the locations for where each item needed to go without one complaint uttered. The inn remained intact. With the work completed, Tessa saw her friends out.

Kierra needed to get on her way to the appointment with Cami and Gavin. Somehow, with Ryan leaning against a bookcase packed with a mix of classic and contemporary novels, and smiling at her, she became clueless on how to put one foot in front of the other and move.

A dash of forgotten optimism stirred within her.

4

*I*n total noncompliance to the No Smoking sign posted in the inn's lobby, the girl exhaled a perfect smoke ring.

Fresh back from her consultation, Kierra halted by the entrance. Amazed, all she could do was to stare.

The stranger wore a loose olive green T-shirt over matching short shorts, clothes Kierra wouldn't have dared worn as a teen, let alone as an adult. With legs draped over an arm of the blue damask armchair, a well-worn sandal dangled from her big toe adorned with a ruby toe-ring, its glitter the only sparkle about her. Long shiny auburn hair fanned the back of the high-back chair.

With images swirling in her mind of her own bold teen years, Kierra swallowed hard. "Hello, there."

The girl fixed her attention on the opposite wall.

Kierra stepped beside her and extended a hand. "There's no smoking inside the inn. For that matter, Kindred Lake Inn is a smoke-free environment. Cig, please."

"It's a free country."

"I do own this property and get to make the rules. Surrender."

Kierra caught an eye roll before the teen complied.

"Thanks." Kierra took off to the kitchen to dispose of the cigarette then hurried back. She didn't have a good feeling about this girl hanging out in the lobby she'd decorated for the comfort of guests...the few she hosted as of late. Her olive drab clothing appeared like moss that covered rock, pretty in its own way but out of place and uninvited. Her heart sagged for this young person without a smile.

Kierra waved away the last remnants of the stale smoke. "That's better. Let's try this again." She smiled widely in an attempt to push aside her growing unease. "My name is Kierra. This place is my home and a place away from home for guests. And you are?"

The girl stared at her black polished fingernails. "Beats me."

This conversation was in a rush to go nowhere. "Well then, how may I help you?"

"No one can help me."

Kierra knelt before the mystery person. "Look at me, sweetie." She waited for the girl's cooperation. After a sour dusting of seconds, she received a sideways glance. Better than nothing.

"Listen, I know I'm in your face, but because you remind me of myself when I was your age, I care about you and want to know what's going on. At least, tell me why you're sitting on my chair as if you run this inn."

"What's the alternative?"

Kierra grinned. "I'll lecture you about the harm you're subjecting your body to by smoking."

"Chill." The girl tucked her chin downward. "It's Bella. And you can own and *operate* this place all you want 'cause I have enough *garbage* to deal with."

Bella was obviously upset and Kierra chose not to react to her word choice of *garbage*. Bella, huh? Where had she heard that name mentioned before?

"I'm waiting for my dad. Like that's not cool anymore?"

Her dad...Bella...Ryan?

"Oh, you're Ryan Delaney's daughter?"

"Yeah. When he remembers."

Those same thoughts about her mother had chiseled away at Kierra's heart for years. Anguish twisted through her as if the hurt was again fresh. With retaliating knees, she stood. "I can relate."

Bella made direct eye contact.

Excellent. Unlike her father's brown eye coloring, hers was a deep forest green. Miles of unexplored paths came to Kierra's mind. Did Ryan and his daughter enjoy walking? Did other trails exist between Ryan and his daughter, like the path of a healing relationship?

"Relate?" Bella said. "How?"

"This whole daughter-parent thing can be a trip at times."

"You're telling me."

"It shouldn't be that way."

Bella turned away, but not fast enough to hide a trembling lower lip.

"Bella?"

"Hey, can you give me space?" She sighed. "I sent my dad a text before my mom dropped me off. He's meeting me any minute."

"Oh, that's nice. Are the two of you going to take advantage of the plenty of nice things to do around town?"

"You sound like a commercial."

"Sorry. Couldn't help it. Tourism runs in my veins." The girl's clipped replies crawled under Kierra's skin. Bella was just a passerby. She didn't need to personally connect with everyone that walked through the inn's front door. Yet, Bella's forlornness plucked an empathetic chord. She studied her possible new friend. The scrawny teen resembled her niece. Both Bella and Zoe had mouths that tended to frown, or smirk at best. Hunched over posture and droop-color clothing screamed keep away.

There was no way she could leave Bella to her own until Ryan showed.

"Do you bike like your dad?"

"Really?"

Hmm. Was that a really, like you think I get into exercising? Or, more like what part of *give me space* don't you get, lady?"

Bella faced her and gave her a lazy grin.

Relief flooded Kierra's chest. She'd push a tad more. "Well?"

"Biking is dad's thing. Not mine, though it wouldn't be far to bike here."

"Oh, do you live close by?"

"Just over the town line, like five miles the most." A look of hesitation crossed Bella's face then disappeared. "I live with my mom. My folks split years ago. Like when I was a kid."

This child before her was still a kid, in need of love and guidance. Then again, wasn't everyone in need of love?

"Thanks for trusting me with your personal story, Bella. My father died years ago, when I was ten, five years after he divorced my mother. Just me, my mom, and my older sister and her daughter. Actually, they moved in with me this morning."

"Cool, I guess."

"I bet you'd like my niece, Zoe." Kierra again looked about the room. Silence ruled, which was definitely not the norm when it came to her family. What was up with that? "I'll introduce you to Zoe. Actually, I'm pretty amazed none of them are around."

Bella dropped a cell phone that Kierra hadn't noticed the girl clutched. In one graceful swoop, Bella stood to retrieve it. A necklace snuck out of her tee and caught in her hair. She groaned. "Nothing ever goes right for me."

"Let me help." Before Bella might object, Kierra combed her fingers in the girl's tangled locks and gently freed a gold cross. She stepped back a few inches to admire the pendant that symbolized eternal life for those who believed in the Father and His Holy Son. "What a lovely cross."

Bella shrugged. "My next door neighbor convinced me and mom to attend her church. Mom is. I'm in the middle of figuring this God stuff out."

"You're not alone. I have some kinks to straighten out in my faith beliefs."

"Say what?"

The front door banged shut.

"There you are," Anna said. "Kierra, I can't believe that you left us alone on our first day? We don't know our way around town, or anyone else."

Kierra hugged her middle as she faced her mother. Anna stood beside the door, refreshed in a change of outfit. The sharp, crisply ironed navy blue pantsuit may have helped to highlight her short-cropped and touched-up blond hair, yet served to shade her facial features a bit on the severe side.

The old feeling of belittlement and insecurity wrapped around Kierra like a jacket three sizes too small. "Mom, I had a business appointment that I had to keep. I'd mentioned it to Tessa. Didn't she tell you?"

Anna waved a hand. "Your sister tells me what she wants when she wants."

"Don't worry lady," Bella said. "You can't get lost in Kindred Lake."

Anna narrowed her eyes. "And you are?"

"None of you—"

"She's my daughter," Ryan called as he bounded down the stairs.

Kierra took in the sight of her new guest. His dark hair freshly washed accented his blue denim shirt and form-fitting black jeans. Aware she was goggling, turning away or for that matter, breathing became a non-option.

"Bella," Ryan said. "If you're set, let's go."

"Where to, Dad?" Bella had put a little oomph behind the word *dad*, though she kept her eyes trained on Anna.

Ryan glanced at his watch. "The rental place should have dropped off a car. Let's check and we'll take it from there."

"There is an additional vehicle." Anna grinned. "I didn't think it was a guest checking into this place."

Kierra wanted to disappear. "Mom...please..."

Ryan rounded the oak newel post and signaled to his daughter. He eyed Anna. "Kierra has one of the most attractive and accommodating inns I've had the pleasure of staying in."

Bella smirked. "Can we stay a few more minutes?"

"Let's go," Ryan said. "I don't have time."

Bella smirk turned downward into a frown. "You always say that."

"Did you hear me?" Ryan approached her, reached out, and enveloped her into a tight hug. "I'm glad to see you again." He mussed her hair.

"Why does everyone mess with my hair?"

"Don't know about others, but I do it because you're cute. Plus, I'm a guy who will forever do guy things without clever explanations. Cool with that?"

"Yeah." She stared hard at him. "I'm cool."

With Ryan's arms wrapped around Bella, they left. Moments later the soft sound of a car starting then crunching over the white pebbly driveway filtered indoors.

"I can't tell if you're more intrigued about the girl or her dad."

Kierra shook her head. "Sorry. What did you say, Mom?"

"Nothing that mattered."

Ryan. He'd reached out and extended his love to his daughter despite her unwelcoming attitude. His behavior might be a good example of how to deal with her own family tension.

Kierra walked straight to her mother, ignored Anna's gasp when she took her hands, and smiled. "I have a pitcher of homemade lemonade in the fridge, or if you'd like I can make you hot tea. Let's settle in the kitchen and catch up." She paused, waiting and hoping her mom would make eye contact, which she did. "I can't wait to hear about your trip."

"Do you mean that?"

"Yes." She smiled at her mom and led her into the kitchen. "Comment away."

Without waiting for an invitation Anna sat at the table. "Why do you always think I have something negative to say?"

Kierra smiled. "You usually have thoughts to share."

"That's a positive spin."

The two chuckled in unison, a nice melodic blend of pitches.

Anna glanced about. "This certainly is a bright, warm kitchen."

Kierra's breath twisted with a pinch of delightful surprise. "You like it?"

"Yes. You've done a nice job making it homey with the bright yellows and greens." Anna's gaze fixed around the small yellow daisy wallpaper pattern against the greenish pasture background. She rubbed her arms. "And I like the professional touches you have."

Her mom didn't *love* the kitchen, but she could easily accept her word choices of *nice* and *like*.

Anna leaned back into her chair in a more relaxed position and pointed to the counter across the room. "That's some gadget."

"You approve of my high-test mixer? I use it making breakfast for my guests."

"I imagine you would. That's what caught my attention when I first walked into the room."

Were they actually conversing? Would her mom ask what kind of things she made? What she enjoyed most about opening her home to others and hosting them as guests? Maybe she'd ask her to name her most memorable visitor or the opposite, a person she hoped never to see again. That included Jonathan. Would she finally ask how she was fairing from the breakup?

Long seconds of waiting spanned between them. Like waiting

for dough to rise, patience wasn't one of her strong assets. She rushed to fill the awkward gap. "My specialty is Scandinavian Danish Bread. Guests always ask for the recipe."

Anna narrowed her eyes. "And you give it to them?"

"Of course."

"There's the problem."

Kierra lifted the beige cloth napkin from the placemat before her and wrung it. "I'm not following you."

"That's why your guests don't return. You're not leaving them wanting more."

"Mom, I don't think you understand about the hospitality business."

Anna pushed back from the table. "I was a food magazine editor before you came along. The high viewership of my popular food blog has made me an award winner. I most definitely understand about the hospitality—"

A door slammed shut and snuffed Anna's words. Zoe's chatter filled the air, followed by another's groan.

"Is that Zoe?" Anna asked. "Sounds like someone else is with her."

"Let's find out. Something is definitely wrong."

5

I wish you weren't my father. This nonsense was worse than any of Ryan's nightmares and scared the life out of him. How could his daughter shout the words he never wanted to hear? To make things more dramatic and frightening, at a red light she'd shoved open the passenger car door, and ran as if her life depended on it.

She was gone. Not a trace of her on either side of the road. He pushed away the achiness cutting through his head. He needed to be levelheaded.

Yeah, right. Forget the calm and sensible approach.

He spun the rental car around. The tires squealed. Good thing traffic wasn't approaching in either direction. Inch by inch he continued to crawl down the road back toward Kindred Lake Inn. He mentally slapped himself for failing to note what his daughter wore or whether she carried a cell phone or wore a hair clip. What kind of father was he?

One who loved his daughter in an abundance he didn't know he was capable of until he saw her born.

He hadn't realized he'd begun driving again and stopped in time when a golden retriever ran across the road followed by a dude barely out of his teens. He stood in front of the car's path with his hands out as if he'd been prepared to stop the vehicle by sheer muscle power if needed.

"Watch it. You totally almost made me and my dog roadkill."

Ryan poked his head out the driver's window. "You see a girl with long brownish red hair?"

The dog owner whistled for his companion. "Rocky, come boy." He swept his uncombed sandy hair from his eyes then patted his thighs. "Rocky, it's okay. Come, buddy."

About to ask for the second time, Ryan snapped his mouth shut when he saw the dog trot back to his owner, tail wagging.

Dog and owner hugged each other. The over-grown teen clipped a leash onto Rocky's collar and stared at Ryan. "The way you drive I can tell you're not from this town. You better be more careful. No wonder why that girl ran from you." He pursed his lips. "Hey, you're not after her in a bad way?"

The question turned Ryan queasy. "No. She's my daughter. She took off on me and I'm trying to find her."

The stranger thumbed over his shoulder. "She might have hit the shops on Main."

"Hey—thanks. Move, so I can."

As soon as Rocky and his owner walked away from the car, Ryan stomped on the accelerator and headed toward the town's business district.

He sped past a Little Bears Day Care and wondered about its attendees. He hoped for forever smiles on their faces...he hoped his own daughter would smile again. He passed Clyde's Hardware Store and grew curious—was anyone named Clyde these days? He might have considered the other assorted shops cute and quaint if on a leisurely stroll with his daughter looking for a place to enjoy a fresh baked treat and a cool glass of iced tea. But, he definitely wasn't on some slowpoke feel-good walk. And surely wasn't at Bella's side.

He turned left and headed out of the downtown area. Businesses slipped by, then houses. Soon enough tall oak and maple trees lined the road, a few posted with trail markers. Bella knew Kindred Lake as if its map spanned intricately throughout her mind. Trouble was, he didn't know squat about the place, or more importantly, much about his daughter. He took that back. The one thing he absolutely knew was her dislike and disapproval of him.

If he could only find her he'd hoped to change things for the better.

Prepared to phone his ex to see if Bella had returned home and then the police if she hadn't, he acted on a hunch. Seconds later, he pulled into Kindred Lake Inn's driveway. If need be, he'd do whatever it took to find his daughter, including search the place from attic to cellar to find her hiding spot.

He stood motionless by the entry. Unsure whether he could trust his eyes, but wanting to believe in the miracle of his daughter safe and secure, he blinked as he absorbed the sight before him. Bella, Kierra and her mom, and Zoe stood side by side with arms linked to form a chain. He was glad for his daughter that she'd met Zoe; the two stood to benefit from each other's company, and possibly friendship. His spirits lifted more when he noted the silly hats they wore. As one, they swayed in sync to a beat only their ears heard.

Kierra's mom patted her red lobster hat. Its big claws jingled. "Let's make wishes."

Kierra, whose luscious figure couldn't be marred by what looked like a single bowling pin stemming from her head, tilted her head but managed to catch the pin before it toppled over. She giggled. "I almost made a strike."

"Oh, brother," Zoe said. Her hat was a white cake with three sparkling candles on top.

"Anyways," Kierra continued, "Instead of wishing, I'll say a praise."

Anna gave a sideways look. "As in thanking God?"

Kierra and the bowling pin bobbed. "Yes. I'm thankful to God that my family is here." She gave Bella a squeeze. "And for my new friend. Yay, Bella."

Bella's hands flew to her hat, a blue, green, orange, and red parrot. "Aw. That's the nicest thing I've heard today."

Anna sniffled loudly. "Doesn't anyone want to hear my wish?"

"I do, Grandma," said Zoe.

"I wish for happiness and new beginnings."

"You're including me?" Bella said.

As he continued to watch, Ryan's heart squeezed with emotion.

"Yes, especially for you and Zoe," Anna said. "You two are the youngest and have a whole future to look forward to."

Kierra swiped her nose with a finger. "You're going to make me cry."

Ryan couldn't stay still a second longer. He wanted to swing a protective arm around his daughter and promise to make her wishes come true, or at least to make her happy. He wanted her to give him another chance.

Bella needed him. He *needed* her.

Kierra turned and smiled at him. As if gorgeous red roses and apricot tulips sprouted around her, beauty accenting beauty, he couldn't turn away. His breathing eased. He hardly knew her, yet when he was within feet of her he was happy and relaxed.

"Ah, we have another partygoer." She waved him over. "Come join the celebration."

With both hands he pointed to his head. "I don't have a hat."

She laughed a whimsical note. "I have one hat left. Check it out."

He hurried over, thankful his daughter watched rather than turned away, or worse, walked away.

From inches behind them, he said, "Hope it's not a jester's hat."

"What's a jester?" Bella asked.

Anna leaned over and whispered into the girl's ear. Bella then murmured a long *oh*.

"You need to read more," Zoe said.

Bella crossed her arms, narrowed her eyes then smirked. "Guess you're right, girlfriend."

Kierra hoisted a large blue sack Ryan hadn't noticed earlier and set it on the mahogany coffee table. "Well, let's see." She winked. "To receive this noble hat, you must stand beside the lass of your choice and wrap an arm around her."

"Lass? What's that?" Bella asked.

"Ha, I know that one too," Zoe said, her tone commiserative.

Anna sighed. "I need to update you two, sweethearts, on old things of yesteryear."

"Whatever," Zoe and Bella said in unison and then giggled.

Ryan went straight to his daughter and wrapped an arm around her. Would she bolt?

Bella leaned into his embrace.

"Here you are." Kierra, standing before him, handed him a hat. "Sorry it's a bit crumpled but it's been in the bottom of this bag for ages."

Ryan unfolded the hat, stared, and laughed. "A tie-dyed hat with a piece sign. How cool is that?"

"Peace?" Bella sniffled against his side. "Totally awesome, Dad."

Over his daughter's shoulder he mouthed a *thank you* to Kierra.

"You're welcome," she said softly.

6

*K*ierra accepted Ryan's offer for a walk alongside Kindred Lake without second thoughts. She had to get out of the inn, away from the craziness. How had a special moment of peace gone wrong as quickly as it did?

"Wait for me," Ryan called from behind.

She slowed her pace until he caught up. "Sorry. I'm fueled by what just happened."

"Fueled or frazzled?"

"Actually, both. I imagine you're also a bit frazzled."

He nodded. "That's what I appreciate about you, Kierra. You're sensitive to others."

"Tell that to Jonathan," she mumbled then slapped a hand over her mouth.

"An ex?"

She gave a little nod. "Sort of. We were engaged. I'm thankfully at the stage that I'm beginning to think he was more an apparition than a real person."

"Sorry to hear it didn't work out."

"It's past tense. You know, life continues on." They continued their walk, side by side. "Want to chill down a bit? We can talk about the large flocks of ducks that declare the lake their own and quack their attitude at people when they also want to enjoy the water. Or, how about the youth group in town that does an awesome job gathering discarded trash from alongside the roads?"

He slipped his hand around hers, his touch a perfect glove of warmth to the otherwise nippy afternoon, and led her to a grassy spot alongside the water. "Would you get chilled if we rested and chatted?"

She doubted she'd be cold anywhere with Ryan. "Thanks for asking. I'll be fine. This is a perfect location, both private and scenic. Well, private that is until the volleyball tournaments start at the end of the month."

"Does Kindred Lake have its own team?"

"You bet, the Ace Punchers. They're ace for a reason."

"Do you play?"

She pointed to herself. "Me? No way. I'm forever traumatized by my middle school gym games."

He laughed, a sound that more and more was becoming music to her soul.

He tugged her to the ground where they lay hip to hip, his fingers laced with hers.

Two geese honked as they flew across the backsplash of a bright blue sky speckled with a few scattered clouds.

"Want to share your thoughts?" he asked.

Kierra smiled. He seemed genuinely interested in her. "One summer, when Tessa was twelve and I was ten, we called ourselves the Lemonade Girls."

He rubbed the top of her hand with his thumb, the touch gentle and comforting. "What's with that name?"

"Mom was always busy. We knew to keep out of trouble, but it was always a question of how. The exciting or the boring way? I suggested we sell lemonade. The twist was to offer the cold drink free to anyone over the age of thirty."

"Thirty?"

"Back then I thought thirty was ancient and that those poor frail elderly folks needed a break in life."

He chuckled.

She relaxed more. "It went well."

"Oh, I imagine it did, especially if it was a hot day."

"It was one long hot summer, but that one successful day encouraged us to try our lemonade stand in various spots around town."

"And the Lemonade Girls became a thriving entity?"

"Most definitely. We made a whole twenty dollars that summer. We were awesome, at least in our minds." She propped onto an elbow. "Thanks for helping me to remember this pleasant memory."

"Good. I'm glad I can do that little for you."

She pointed at a chubby cloud floating by. "Have you ever likened a cloud shape to a dog, a snowman, or what have you?"

"Ten years ago on July 4th."

"Whoa. You didn't hesitate with that date."

He looked away for a moment. When he faced her again, distinct pain shadowed his eyes. She inched her fingers up to feather them across his check to push away his hurt, but then pulled back. This was crazy. She didn't know him. Had no business touching him in an intimate way.

With Jonathan's exit two years ago she didn't want nor need another partner in her life. Besides, business-wise, he was a guest in her inn. They had a natural boundary made of distinct roles that neither should cross.

"That day I could never forget, Kierra."

She loved how her name rolled easily from his mouth, a sound that conjured in her mind fields of wild flowers, choruses of birdsong, and smiling faces.

In total contradiction to her resolve to respect their boundaries, she fanned her fingertips on his upper arm. Like a butterfly discovering the sweet nectar of a blossom, she didn't want to flit away.

"What happened?"

"On that Fourth of July I'd cloud-watched with Bella. Lisa, my then wife, and I just had an awful fight and I found Bella sobbing behind the couch."

"Oh, if this is too personal and bittersweet there's no need to share."

"Actually, I'd like to." He squeezed her hand. "That's when we lived together in Maryland. I wanted to erase the tears from my little girl's face, on a forever level. We went out for chocolate soft serve ice cream cones with red, white, and blue sprinkles for the holiday. She then asked if we could go to the community park and there was no way I could refuse. With contented full bellies, we stretched across a grassy slope and took turns declaring cloud shapes."

"Remember a particular one?"

He lifted onto an elbow as well, his face mere inches from hers. "I saw a cloud formation of a brick wall; Bella saw a teddy bear. No psychology degree necessary to figure that one out."

"How did things go the rest of that summer?"

"Not well. I came home from work early one day and discovered—in our bedroom—why Lisa wanted an out from our marriage." He squinted as if the whole scene flashed before him. "The speed of covering themselves and their shame up with the bed sheets must have broken a world record. Their excuses were pitiful."

Kierra moaned. "That's awful."

"Yep. The divorce was mutual. Because of my job demands Lisa got custody of Bella, but I had complete visitation rights as well as Bella staying with me whenever she wanted. Four years ago Lisa took Bella and moved to the Kindred Lake area. She lives with her fiancé, Alex."

"The same one you...uh...caught?"

"Thankfully no."

Kierra wanted to ask more. What choices did Bella make? Had Lisa tainted their daughter's young mind with untruths about her father? Was Lisa a good mom? Instead, she held back. With his hurts apparently raw, Ryan needed space.

"Ah, I get why you came here on your vacation."

He narrowed his eyes; his face remained poker-faced blank. "Don't assume, Kierra. It might be that I'm in town to check out the rumors of the pretty innkeeper."

She recognized his sweet tease, yet her cheeks burned. "Well, if you ever need a shoulder to lean on, I'm here for you."

His eyes sparkled as if they'd smiled. "Thank you."

She sat, hugging her knees. He did the same.

"I'm not on vacation."

She hadn't expected him to say that. "Pardon?"

He waved his hand. "Nothing."

"Well then, sorry about my sister making a mess of things when she barged in and found the five of us goofing with our hats on. She's been on edge as of late. We were enjoying a good time, that's all."

"More like we were letting go of a few hurts."

Seated on the grass beside Ryan, Kierra shook the unpleasant recollection from her mind of her sister's overreaction to them playing around with the hats. "Do you ever wish there was a way to silence the noise of ugliness when it's your own family causing the problem?"

"Definitely."

"Any suggestions on how?"

Their hands rested side by side. She grasped his and watched as a smile lifted his beautiful lips.

"The same as I've done since Bella was born...keep loving her. And praying she'll recognize and accept my love sooner than later."

"Is that praying as in wishing for the cosmos to work or praying as in talking to God?"

"Let's just say God and I chat a lot." He lifted their hands to his lips and kissed the back of her hand. And flinched. "Sorry."

"Why would you be sorry?"

He looked at their linked hands. "My kiss. It wasn't inappropriate?"

She smiled softly. "Good question."

---

7

*F*ive busy days sped by since Kierra and Ryan exchanged concerns over both the past and present. Kierra didn't know what to think about Ryan. She understood and admired how he spent extra time with his daughter and then biked off by himself. Perhaps he needed personal space to relax and think about things. Yet, his sweet kiss to her hand while they had cloud gazed had left an indelible mark, as if she could still feel the touch of his lips.

As for her family, Kierra hoped they'd entered a settle-down mode. Tessa enrolled Zoe in the middle school, thankful that Bella could ease her way by showing her around the campus and introduce her to classmates. Her sister also put in a few job applications about town. Her mom resumed her blog and kept occupied. When she found Anna folding a white blouse in the laundry room off of the kitchen and humming an old Doris Day movie musical tune, she hummed in joy right along with her mother.

"Nice to see you're making yourself at home, Mom."

Anna placed the garment on top of the washing machine. "Is that sarcasm or sincerity?"

A handful of responses flooded Kierra's mind. One rose above the others and pushed its way out of her mouth before she had a second to reconsider. "It saddens me, Mom, that you don't know me well enough to gauge where I'm coming from." Ryan's words came to her...how he kept trying to communicate with his daughter while continuing to pray for her. And here she was, in defense mode. That attitude would only serve to maintain the barriers between them.

"Sorry, Mom."

Anna's brows knotted. "About what?"

"About reacting emotionally. I came off like a whiny little girl."

Anna smoothed the blouse that didn't need additional straightening. "I shouldn't have pushed you, should have simply accepted your comment about me making myself at home for what it was."

"Want some tea or a snack?"

"I can find my way around in a kitchen." Anna groaned. "I'm making things worse. My specialty lately."

Kierra patted her mom's arm. "Let's go into the kitchen, shall we?"

"Sounds good."

Once inside Kierra's favorite room, she gestured toward the table. "Have a seat. What would you like? I know you enjoy tea, hot or cold, and bought a variety. There's also assorted fresh fruit and though I baked the batch of pumpkin muffins for tomorrow's breakfast, there are a couple to spare." Amazed her mom hadn't interrupted her babbling she glanced at her then wished she hadn't when she saw Anna's pursed lips.

Kierra tried to ignore her tight insides. Her conversation with Ryan, a perfect stranger, had gone smoother than this attempted chat with her own mother. "I can't tell what you're thinking."

"Does it matter?"

Again Ryan's words came to her. He prayed in hope that Bella would accept his love for her. She needed to pray as well and there was no better time than the present. Without second thoughts she turned to face the counter and leaned into it. She rested her eyes shut to block out her surroundings and to focus her heart on the Father she hadn't spoken to in a while. *Lord, I know you blessed me with the mom I have for a reason and I thank you. Help us to love each other.*

A chair scraped the floor.

She pivoted around. She'd forgotten her mother was seated at the table. "Mom? Don't leave. I want your company."

"The way you turned your back I thought you wished me away."

"Just the opposite."

"That's good to know," Anna said softly. She slid the chair under the table. "I'll settle on a cup of hot tea. Hold off on those high-caloric muffins."

"For you, I'd substituted applesauce for the butter. Less fat."

"Then I'll indulge in one tomorrow morning. Thanks, anyway."

"An apple or a handful of red grapes?"

"I'm fine. I'll save my appetite for dinner."

"Mom, for better or worse, my curiosity is flaring up. What's on your mind?"

"You do like playing with matches." Anna sighed dramatically. "I taught you better."

Kierra stiffened.

"Relax. I'm teasing."

Kierra poured tap water into the kettle and lit a gas burner. "I'm listening."

"Funny, I always enjoy hearing that click-click of a stovetop igniting."

"I agree." The tension in Kierra's shoulders eased. "Looks like we have something in common besides genes."

Anna shook a finger in a playful manner. "Now, who is teasing whom?"

"Mom, you're stalling."

"I am, indeed." Anna moved the china bowl filled with sugar from the table's center toward her placemat then slid it back. "Sorry, sweet stuff. Sadly, I don't need you," she said to the bowl's contents then glanced back at Kierra. "What was brewing in my mind was a huffy-puffy tirade about how I know my way around the kitchen. Totally inappropriate."

Her mom was confessing to curbing one of her infamous outbursts? Kierra faced the cabinet where she kept the coffee mugs and teacups and saucers. *Thank you, God.* She reached toward another cupboard where she kept the tea.

Anna groaned. Two groans in what, a span of three minutes? Can't be good.

"What now?" Kierra asked as gently as she could.

"You might not want to open that door."

"I have no choice if you want tea." Without hesitation she pulled open the cabinet. And laughed.

"I couldn't help it."

She turned. "Mother. Really? You had to group the teas by box color?"

Anna chuckled then covered her mouth. "It's better than what I did inside your other cabinets."

"Oh, no. Did Super Organizer strike again?"

"I left my cape upstairs." Anna burst out in a hearty laugh.

Kierra opened the food pantry in the corner of the room. Yep. The canned and jarred goods were alphabetized from artichokes to jalapeños and right through to the packages of soba noodles. She joined her mom's goose-like cackle.

"Sweetheart," Anna said. "You know me when I step into a kitchen."

Kierra reached for a pastel pink teacup. Pink was her mom's

favorite color and it didn't escape her that she wanted to please her. She steeped the sweet berry tea with the hot water.

"And no one invited me to this little get-together?" Tessa said as she entered the kitchen. Her tan slacks and white blouse a notable moderation on the loud colors she preferred.

Anna rocked back, surprise flashing across her face. "When was the last time I told you that you have poor timing?"

Tessa glanced at her watch. "About two hours ago."

Kierra snorted. "Have a seat, sis. Want a soda? How about a sweet?"

"No, thanks. I've begun a no-sugar diet. I decided that if I'm making a new start in life in a different location, I'm going to be good to my body as well. Maybe I'll manage to shed a few pounds before I fill out more job applications."

"Good for you, not that you have a spare pound to lose, but I'm glad you want to take care of your health. Water, then?"

Tessa nodded and sat opposite of their mom. She set her cell phone on the placemat before her.

Anna wrapped her fingers around the teacup. "Anyways, what I was trying to admit is that I've been more bossy over the years rather than motherly."

Tessa didn't reply.

"Actually, for that matter, I've failed to be tender as well." Anna looked at Tessa then Kierra. "Do you two think it's too late for me to start?"

"It's never late," Tessa said tenderly. She began to rub her temples.

"Tessa, dear," Anna said. "What's wrong?"

"Headache coming on."

On her feet before anyone asked, Kierra searched for aspirin in the cabinet over the sink. She held back what would have been an out of place chuckle when she noted her over-the-counter remedies had also been arranged alphabetically. "Here you go. Extra strength." She offered the aspirin to Tessa. "We're supposed to get rain tomorrow. Is the change in barometric pressure getting to you?"

"Weather doesn't bother me like it does you," Tessa said, flashing a questionable eye at Kierra. She chugged down the two aspirin dryly.

"Oh, I forgot to give you the water," Kierra said.

Tessa waved her off. "Not a big issue. Chalk off my throbbing head to an upset daughter."

Kierra sat beside her sister. Gently, she rubbed her back. "Where's Zoe?"

"The last I know she's with Bella. Don't ask me where, though. Haven't a clue. It's Saturday and two teen girls are off conquering the world."

"Is that what's upsetting you?" Kierra asked.

Tessa shook her head then groaned, and rubbed again at her temples. "There's a lot on my mind."

A rap came at the kitchen's entrance.

"May I join you, or would you like your privacy?" Ryan asked.

Kierra's focus shouldn't have left her mom and sister, yet she couldn't deny how fast her attention riveted to Ryan. Casual and relaxed looking in blue jeans and a black denim shirt, he appeared as if he belonged in her kitchen, beside her. "Please, do keep us company."

"Have a seat." Tessa pulled out the chair next to her. "Would you know where the girls are?"

"If you pardon me, I have a blog post to work on." Anna winked twice. "Besides, you don't need this old fogey around. Let me know about Zoe and Bella, but they're likely out and having fun."

"Oh, Mom," Kierra said, delighting in the words she was about to say. "You're welcome to stay."

"Yes," Ryan said. He'd taken a seat next to Tessa but rose. "Please don't leave on my account."

"Stay seated, Ryan. There's always work to be done, and I like to stay busy." Anna gave a warm smile then left the room.

"I haven't a clue to where Bella and Zoe are," Ryan said. "Quite vexing, especially since I'm Bella's dad and should know. I was hoping they'd be here."

The front door slammed shut.

Kierra stood. "With doubt that's a new guest, that must be the girls."

Tessa called their names.

"Told you we'll be sorry for showing up," Bella said seconds before entering the kitchen. Zoe followed. Both wore their long hair in ponytails with matching red bands, their glistening locks a peek at youth at its best.

Ryan pulled out two chairs. "Sit now, please."

Pale-faced and serious, the teens exchanged shrugs.

"That's correct," Ryan added. "Not an option, especially when you both know better than to disappear without telling us where you're going, let alone failing to ask for permission."

"What?" Zoe said with a distinct whine. "Like you're my dad? And I have to report to you?"

Tessa patted Zoe's arm. "Cool it. Ryan's right. You do know better."

Bella scanned each adult's face. "You'll be cool with this part —we actually went to the library. But when we got there we checked out a fire in a trashcan in front of the library."

"More like checked out the awesome looking firemen when they arrived," Zoe said.

Bella flashed her cell phone, a big grin spreading across her face. "We called 911, and of course then went into the library to alert the staff. You know, it could have gotten out of hand, like the fire jumping to the library. That old building is made of wood." She set the phone down and splayed her hands on the table's surface. "It would have gone pop and bye real fast. Are you proud of us, Dad? I did good for a change."

"I am proud. You did the right thing." Ryan pulled at his chin. "Since you arrived before anyone else, did you see who set the fire?"

Bella jumped to her feet. "That's so like you, Dad. Not trusting me. I bet you think it was us that set the fire."

"I didn't say a word about trust."

"You didn't have to. It's in your eyes."

"Bella, please listen."

"No." Bella began backing out of the kitchen toward the hallway. "I've had enough of your stupid reporter ways."

Ryan stood. "Where are you heading?"

"I'm going back to Mom's, where I belong." Bella ran from the room.

"I'll go with you," Zoe said.

Tessa grabbed her daughter by the elbow. "Stay put."

"Mom..."

"Zoe, for once don't give me an argument. Do as I say."

"Why?"

Tessa pulled her into a tight embrace and sniffled. "Because, I love you."

"Excuse me," Ryan said. "I'm stepping outdoors in need of fresh air."

"Are you going after Bella?" Kierra asked.

He shook his head. "Not quite yet. I'll phone and make sure she arrives at her mom's, and give her a chance to drop the drama. This isn't the first time this has happened between us."

"Want my company?"

"I'd appreciate that. Do you have a bike?"

"Not a top-notch one like yours. But hey, it has wheels."

His eyes brightened. "Let's go, then."

8

*R*yan glanced over his shoulder and scolded himself, thankful Kierra couldn't hear. Here they were, bicycling together down a path alongside the lake, except he, on his fancy schmancy bike, had left her trailing behind by at least a hundred feet. What was his problem? Well, other than one upset daughter on his mind?

He slowed to a barely pedaling pace. She caught up.

"It's about time," he called out, playfully.

"You're a cyclist rock star." With an exaggerated swipe of hand, she wiped her brow. "Some of us in the real world don't have the slick bicycle, let alone the perfectly toned, muscular body to pump those tires."

They both stopped. And stared at each other.

He cracked a smile he'd never expected possible given the current situation with Bella. "You think?"

A flush stamped her face apple red, yet she smiled.

Confident, despite the sweet colorful hue. He liked that about her. "You look even more prettier when you blush."

She slid her hands across her face. "Did I say what I think I did?" she said with a smile in her voice. "Wait a second. Did you just say what I thought I heard?"

"You did, and yes, I did. Indeed. Know what?"

She moved her fingers an inch on her face and peeked at him. "Do I want to know?"

"You also have one fine body as well, one I haven't been able to stop admiring since I first set my eyes on you." He wondered if he needed to clarify that. "Nor do I want to stop this delight."

"Delight, huh?" She giggled. "You sound a tad old-fashioned."

"Disappointed?"

"No way. I like what's before me." With hands entirely off her face, she gave him a slow perusal then surprised him by moving alongside him and grabbing the handlebars of his bike. "But we both know this isn't the time or place for sweet talk."

He winked. "We could ignore our conscience."

"You're the one when it came to my family troubles, steered me to God. I can't imagine your sole focus is on pleasure."

He snapped his fingers. "Drats. I was hoping."

She giggled again.

"You have a lovely laugh."

"Oh, stop." She lifted her chin toward the iron railing alongside the path. "Let's hang out there for a few minutes—it's not a high traffic area. I think we need to talk about a few things."

"What's it to you, my pretty innkeeper?"

She batted her lashes. "What flattery. Nope, won't work on me, my hunky athlete."

"What flattery," he said, repeating her words and matching her syrupy tone. "Although, since I'm not used to hearing the word hunky connected to me, I'm not complaining. Why do you want to bother talking with me? I'm essentially a stranger."

"Because I care."

He pointed at his chest and mouthed, "About me?"

"And the more I'm with you the more I'm liking you." She clutched his fingers and swung their joined hands between them.

"I can't believe no woman has ever linked you with the description of hunky."

"I've definitely been called many things, but that term isn't one of them."

"What's wrong with the world?"

The answer lingered between them. They moved onto the trail's shoulder where they leaned the bikes against the railing. He rested against the metal barrier, legs stretched before him. She distanced herself a foot away.

"This won't do." He inched closer until their hips touched. "Much better."

"Yes, it is."

Her voice was luscious and soft, and he had to restrain from swinging his arm around her. Instead, he looked straight ahead and asked, "Where should we begin this conversation?"

"Bella stirred my curiosity about you when she said that thing about you being a reporter. I tend to mind my own business, tend to give others a lot of space, but I get this feeling that what brought you to Kindred Lake may not have been a good thing." She paused for a beat or two. "I hope it isn't ruining things between you and your daughter. Family ties are often fragile and I'd hate for you not to enjoy this time together."

He faced her. "And you surmised this from when Bella alluded to my, quote, stupid reporter ways?"

"Yes. Was she referring to a local neighborhood small rag or larger, like The Baltimore Sun?"

"Bella has this way of downplaying things, especially when it comes to her old man. Try the news anchor at the lead Baltimore station."

"Seriously?"

He nodded.

"Hmm. I guess I can picture you in a suit and tie."

As her smile grew, his faded. She might be trying her best to ease the tension, yet he folded within himself as if an origami figure. But rather than becoming a piece of artwork he shrank tiny and dark.

"You don't look happy." She surprised him by wrapping an arm around his shoulders. "May I ask what happened?"

He rubbed at the pinch between his brows, his body's go-to spot of tension. "It's complicated."

"Of course it is. Life tends to be messy at one point or another."

"A big amen on that one."

She waited. In the past if someone had pushed him he tended to clam up. With Kierra he wanted to share.

He breathed in deeply and exhaled slowly. "As a news junkie, I volunteered as an unpaid intern while in high school at a small local station. I worked hard and began to climb the journalistic food chain ladder in the newsroom. While in college I worked part-time as an equivalent to a newspaper stringer—an independent in the thick jungle of the news arena."

With her eyes focused on the ground, she pressed down on her bottom lip. He appreciated her good listening skills. Seldom did others take two seconds to give an attentive ear.

"I stuck with it," he continued. "Year after year. Good days. Rotten ones. The broadcasting gods of the station fit and molded me into the news anchor of their dreams until another offer came along, cue the bigger station. I ran with it."

"I haven't watched the Maryland stations, yet I definitely have heard of you. Just didn't connect the name to the person." She flashed him a foxy grin. "That's a good thing. Otherwise, I probably would have gone fangirl crazy over you and made a fool of myself."

"I'm thinking it's impossible for you to do that."

"The fool part? Others have differing opinions."

He narrowed his eyes. "Big mistake if you listen to them."

She gave a slow nod. "Since I've been running my own business and getting back on my feet post-Jonathan, I'm discovering that. Enough with me. I also recall your name connected to a few prestigious awards in journalism. Correct?"

This was the second time she'd uttered Jonathan's name. Yet, he knew it wasn't the right time to ask. "Yes to those awards."

She waited. He remained silent.

"I see there's no ego to contend with. I'm glad about that." She offered a soft smile, although that faded. "But, I'm suspecting there's a sad story."

He glanced away. "As we say in the biz, a breakout story."

"I have two good ears and though my shoulders are tiny, they're supportive if you'd like to share. If not, I understand."

He faced her, grateful to again set his eyes on this special woman. "Do you recall the Back Alley Fire stories that broke the news last year?"

She gasped. "Oh, yes. Horrific and tragic."

"Day after day we'd sent our best reporters to cover the fires that began in Maryland's back alleys. They quickly spread from garbage cans and abandoned vehicles to businesses and homes."

She wrapped an arm around her middle and rocked forward. "Weren't ten businesses and about twenty-five houses total losses?"

"Good memory." He paused to let the flash of smoke, sirens, and screams rip through his mind and exit. "The list of suspects ran dry. The lack of witnesses didn't help either. Frustrated, I stormed out of the newsroom determined to investigate the scene myself."

"Any answers?" she asked, her tone but a murmur.

"No." He closed his eyes tight, but it didn't help. In his mind's eye he saw the child, he heard her cry, he inhaled the stench of death. "When I got downtown I walked for hours and became the sole witness to the one perp everyone was looking for, but he got away. The authorities are still searching for him."

A squeeze came to his shoulder. He opened his eyes and looked at her lovely face and kind eyes.

"What did you see?" she asked.

Words clogged his mouth. Again. The same mouth unable to open before a camera.

She waited.

He knew she'd wait forever...for him. In full trust, he swallowed hard and made himself go on.

"Out of nowhere comes this hoodie-wearing ragged person—I couldn't see a face but my gut says it's a he. He grabs a little girl away from her mom in a crowd of onlookers and..."

Kierra pulled him tight to her side.

"And runs. I give chase, screaming at him to drop her. He does, into the flames and flees. She was only four years old."

Kierra began to shake. "What was her name?"

He willed his composure solid. Enough with him. Kierra was distraught. He needed to comfort her. "Emma Lulu," he said softly, wiping her tears with a gentle swipe of his fingertips.

"What an adorable name." She pressed his fingers against her flushed cheeks.

The child's baby blue eyes flashed before him and again he gulped. "She is...was adorable. Her mom was a mess. I imagine she still is."

"Understandably. And you, my friend?"

"I was besides myself for quite a while. Unfortunately, others are seeing me as a professional wreck...that kind of stigma stays fastened on a person like a collar on a dog."

"Did the station terminate you?"

"No, I left. Since I haven't been able to open my mouth before cameras, I hightailed it out of there on a mutually agreed upon hiatus. I've spent the time on my bike in a major chill-out zone. It took a while to accept, but I've reached the conclusion that if good were to come out of this mess I needed to repair my relationship with my daughter before I, like Emma Lulu's mom, lost my little girl. And here I am, in Kindred Lake to love and cherish Bella. Yet, she doesn't want a thing to do with me."

"If I'd witnessed what you had, I'd be trapped in a place of mind I couldn't get out."

"Bella knows about what happened, but you're the only one I'd ever been able to tell. I couldn't even tell my buddy Zander every detail."

"I'm glad you're comfortable with me to share."

"You, Kierra, are the first person I'm relaxed enough with to confide in." He brushed her lips with his. With desire fueled from neither of them pulling back, he pressed further into a kiss that took him to a place he never wanted to return from.

9

*R*yan's kiss carried her to places she'd rather be any day. A barefoot walk on a beach along the Atlantic following sandpiper tracks. Watching fireworks streak the night sky from the top of a Ferris wheel. The flash of reds, oranges, and browns while dancing slow-style with a man she loved while under an autumn tree showering its leaves like confetti.

The memory of Jonathan's words tapped her on the shoulder. *This isn't going to work... let's end it before either of us gets hurt.*

Kierra groaned and pulled away from Ryan. "Sorry. I know better than that."

"Than what? Sharing a kiss?"

"Sharing a kiss with you." It took boosted willpower to keep from leaning toward him for more. "Believe me, if you weren't a guest in my inn we wouldn't be talking about this subject."

"You have a strict no-messing with guests policy?"

She pushed back her hair from her face. "Yes, as a matter of fact, I do."

A few seconds slipped by in silence.

He stood. "You're right. It should be that way."

Although that was the reply she expected, it wasn't the answer she wanted.

He motioned toward their bikes then at the path. "Shall we?"

"And pretend nothing happened between us just now?"

The corners of his eyes drooped. "Did it?"

Yeah, they'd shared a kiss. Fireworks sparked on her end. Had nothing happened for him? Maybe he was politely obliging her work ethics of keeping business just that, business and not crossing that obtrusive line. She had the right to define how she conducted work. That was what she wanted, right?

She walked her bike onto the path. "Yes, let's head back."

Without waiting for a response she swung a leg over the bike's frame and saddled the seat. About to kick off, she heard him calling her name. Like a suave Frenchman out of her dreams, Ryan's silky-voice was the quintessence of attraction to her ears. That was her trouble, crushing on someone she couldn't have.

She turned around.

His chocolate brown eyes may have lost their glint of minutes ago, yet a soft smile awaited her. "Thanks for listening, Kierra."

She nodded. "I hope it helped."

"Definitely." He mounted his bike and zipped past her. "Catch up. I want you beside me."

The first two miles back to the inn was bearable as long as Kierra didn't focus on her out-of-shape, burning leg muscles. The reassurance Ryan rode beside her removed the sting of the tension that had followed their kiss. When they reached the fork in the road where a turn to the right led to the inn another half mile further, and a left took one on a continued scenic route around the lake, everything changed. At the last second, and without a word of explanation, Ryan surprised her when he veered down the picturesque path. Cold seeped through her veins as if a bucket of icy sludge was dumped over her head, soaking her to the bone.

Things will be okay. Keep pumping those pedals.

Just get back to the inn.

As she passed the post office and the old-fashioned mom-and-pop country store neighbors ran, she lifted her head in confidence. The affirmations rolled in. She was a good, kind woman. She'd handled the situation well with Ryan. A woman of integrity, it was wise not to develop a romantic interest with a client. Those things never worked out for the best. Plus, she was barely over Jonathan. She didn't need to jump from one sad relationship into another that had no business starting in the first place.

Then there was the most important proclamation slash mantra she'd vowed when her mom, sister, and niece moved in with her: Family first.

As she pedaled the last few feet of the long circular driveway and spotted Cami's car, relief wrapped her like a warm fuzzy blanket's promise of comfort. As if her friend had sensed Kierra needed sympathetic companionship, she sat behind the driver's wheel before the inn's door, waiting. Anna and Tessa flocked around the blue vehicle.

Kierra headed straight toward the car's rolled down window. "Am I glad to see you."

"Hey, gal. Gavin and I have agreed about the wedding ceremony suggestions you made and"—she held up a stapled bundle of sheets—"I have a signed contract."

"Great."

"Also, I want to run by you this fiddler that came highly recommended. You know how I love the lush tunes that carry me away to simpler and brighter times. His name is Brodie Sullivan. Heard of him?"

"No," Kierra said. "But I'll look into hiring him for you."

"That would be wonderful, and save me heaps of time.

Thanks." Cami's smile faded, her forehead furrowed. "I'm babbling. What's wrong, sweetie? You're looking a bit ruffled since I last saw you."

"More like plain old awful if you ask me," Tessa said.

Kierra steeled a sideways look at her sister.

Tessa lifted her hands, palm side out in surrender, and slowly backed away from the car. "Come on, Mom. Let's go look for my daughter...if I still have one."

"She'll be fine." Anna came around the car and swung an arm around Tessa. "Together, we'll find her. Let's go look."

"Thanks, Mom. You know, I appreciate how you're trying to be easier going with us." They started down the drive.

"Phone my cell if you need me," Kierra called out. "I'll be there for you."

Tessa signaled okay.

Kierra leaned into the vehicle. "Cami, has my mom and sister said anything to you about my niece?"

"From what your mom described, I believe Zoe is fine. Just walking off a dump truck load of teenage angst."

Kierra got teen turmoil and melodrama. Not good. "I hate stuff like this."

"Like what?" Cami said gently.

Cami wasn't being dense. She was giving Kierra space to articulate her own anxiety. She thought about her friend's relationship with her own mom, and how falling in love with Gavin helped to bring her and her mom closer. If anyone, Cami understood where she was coming from.

"Family issues." Kierra stifled a sigh. "I'm trying to be patient with my mom and sister. Know why?"

"Because you love them. Because you want to be loved by them."

Kierra gave a little nod then turned. Cami didn't need to see her eyes misting.

A touch came to her arm. "Those weepy emotions you have are healthy. Let them out."

Who was she fooling? Kierra faced her friend. "And subject you to my craziness?"

"Definitely. How about if we go on a walk?" She winked. "We'll have ourselves a good girls' chat. Life isn't centered on me or my wedding plans."

Kierra eyed the wedding agreement. "What about the paperwork?"

"It's not going anywhere." Cami chuckled. "Neither is Gavin nor myself. We're getting hitched forever and at your lovely Kindred Lake Inn."

"You're beaming."

"You bet I am. Love's a wonderful blessing."

Cami was out and out glowing in love. Her first marriage was a bittersweet relationship of joy and sadness. Her husband had a few emotional problems, but she stood beside him the best she could until his passing. Then Cami and Gavin, ironically old enemies from their high school days, re-met when he became her neighbor. He fell hard and deeply in love with Cami and her son, Danny.

Kierra's eyes flooded with another round of tears.

Cami's smile disappeared. "Oh, no. I'm sorry. I should have kept quiet."

"You're fine. I'm truly happy for you and Gavin."

Cami grasped her hand. "You're not over Jonathan...and I knew better than to yap about falling in love."

"I believe it's more a case of not being over what might have been." Kierra purposely put a smile in place. "Life goes on. Let's go on that walk, shall we?"

"The lake?"

"Of course." Kierra glanced over her shoulder toward the back of the inn where they could easily reach the lake. She smiled at her friend. "Let's first walk down the road a ways. I can use an extra bunch of minutes with you."

They strolled down past the garden, which Kierra had planted in hope it brought to guests' minds English cottages teeming with bright and fragrant blossoms. Jonathan, of course, had to quip that he could always rely on the flowers to trigger a sneezing attack and therefore couldn't appreciate them. Jonathan and Ryan were vastly different from each other. Her former fiancé had an average build, thinning blond hair, and a penchant for slacks and collared long sleeve shirts, whereas Ryan fit nicely into her English garden fantasies. His firm athletic body, a full head of thick dark hair that added a mysterious and suave look, and clothes preferences that shouted a love for the outdoors played nicely in her mind.

Cami giggled. "Did you hear a word I said?"

Heat flushed Kierra's cheeks. Actually, it was likely the whole shebang, from foot to toe. She let a few seconds tick by to collect her wits. "Honestly? No. Sorry."

At the roadside, they turned left toward Kindred Lake.

"You're fine, Kierra. Stop apologizing."

"Mom says I over-apologize."

Cami smiled at two chipmunks playing tag. "Your mother might be onto something. Ever think about bumping up the bold-thingy a notch?"

With the risks she'd taken with Jonathan, she'd certainly been on a brazen streak. "I guess I've mellowed a wee bit these past couple of years since…" She trailed off, not waning to say Jonathan's name or the situation that sparked the unexpected change in her life. It was time to change the subject anyways.

They approached a narrow dirt trail lined with thick bushes. "Be careful not to brush alongside these overgrown weeds. The ticks are bad this year. Seems like every other person I know has come down with Lyme disease."

"Oh, how I know. It's awful. And with this early spring, despite the cool temps, it's nearly epidemic proportions."

Once beside the water Cami breathed in deeply. "My son and I love this lake. We've walked the two-mile length and back several times."

"Wow. Not bad for an eight-year-old boy...and his ancient mom."

"I didn't hear that last part." Cami peered reflectively at the lake. "I'm thankful Gavin enjoys the outdoors. Here, by the lake, the three of us have talked about everything from space aliens to the merits of watching movie musicals."

"I'm thinking Gavin's the one for scary movies?"

"No way. He's the song and dance fanatic and Danny and I can't get enough horror. Well, pretend horror. As long as it's not the real deal."

"I hear you."

A flock of geese honked. They both glanced at the sky.

"I love spring," Kierra said.

Cami eyed her. "Hate to say this, friend, but you don't sound nor look like you're enjoying a thing. And you know what? I don't blame you."

Those words of commiseration soothed Kierra's frazzled feelings. "Thanks," she murmured.

"Tell me where you'd zoned out to minutes ago back by the garden."

"Avoiding the issue of my family moving in by..."

"Yes?"

Kierra smiled at her wise and gentle friend. "By first thinking about Jonathan."

"Ugh."

She grinned. "My thoughts then drifted to Ryan. Well, I admit, more like sprinted to him."

"And he's...?"

"Oh, no one. Just an inn guest."

"And I'm nobody's fool." Cami gently spun Kierra around until they faced each other. "Your eyes didn't sparkle with obvious joy until you mentioned Ryan by name. He may be the ticket out of the Jonathan-blues."

"Cami, he's staying at the inn. You know I don't get involved with guests."

"Considering most of your male clients are age seventy and above, happily rotund, and are in Kindred Lake visiting their grandkids, it's no wonder you've set this policy of yours." She elbowed Kierra playfully in the side. "What's wrong with a little romance? Ha. For that matter, a lot of romance?" She started to hum *Here Comes the Bride.*

"These days I'm wary of roses and hearts. From what I gather from Ryan, it's the wrong time in his life as well. He wants to mend his strained relationship with his daughter." Kierra glanced over her shoulder, half hoping to see her mother or sister waving her over with relieved smiles from finding Zoe and likely Bella, and half hoping she wouldn't see the pair, that she'd have time alone with her friend.

"Is Ryan worth the attention in the looks department?"

"Let's just say he arrived at the inn on his bicycle in form fitting spandex that accented his features on the side of girl eye candy."

"Ooh la la."

Kierra fixed her hands on both hips. "Did I hear you—a reputable preschool director—say what I believe you did?"

"Absolutely," Cami said. She laughed the sweet laugh Kierra always adored. "I ace at taking care of little children, but I'm a grown woman looking forward to making my soon-to-be husband happy." She worried her lips. "Honey, it's time to let go of Jonathan. You've already said goodbye to him, now let him go from your heart."

Kierra shrugged. "I don't know...what about my family? I mean, dealing with the fact that they've moved in with me?"

Cami shook her head. "Wow. That was a quick segue. You do have a lot on your shoulders." She pulled Kierra into a hug.

"Thanks, my friend. I needed that."

"Find another word."

Kierra lifted a brow.

"You used the word deal, as in *dealing with the fact.* Stop dealing with family and start loving them. You deal with phone solicitors; you treasure family. Get it?"

"Ryan has said the same thing, more or less."

"Smart. I already like him. I must meet him, and I know Gavin would as well."

"I'll introduce you."

"Another thing—a big one—pray. Talk more with God. Listen to what He has to say."

"Ryan says he talks often with God."

"I knew he was a decent man."

"But we...he went..." How could she tell her friend that Ryan had parted from her minutes after they'd kissed? Had she misread him?

Maybe Ryan wasn't as *incredible* as she first thought.

Her insides clenched like a fist.

"Hey," came a shout from behind.

They both turned to see Tessa waving frantically for them to come closer.

Already shaky, Kierra braced herself. "This can't be good."

"Pray," Cami said. She grasped Kierra's hand. "I'm right beside you."

"Hurry," called Tessa. "We have a situation."

10

---

*T*essa puffed out a long breath. "We found the girls."

Kierra looked at Tessa's empty car then back at her sister. "Great news. Where are they?"

Tessa stared at the ground.

"Want me to give you some privacy?" Cami asked.

"Oh, no," Tessa said. "You're fine."

"When you shouted at me mere seconds ago you sounded pretty upset," Kierra said. "What's this about a situation? Start from the beginning."

Tessa leaned against the car. "First, you need to chill."

Kierra's past go-to reaction toward her sister might have been to bristle, but what she sensed the most was that Tessa needed her support, not petty antagonism about her choice of words. She also remembered what Cami had said about praying more.

And Ryan believed in talking with God.

Father, my life is in your Mighty hands and I trust You.

"You're right." She aimed for a gentler tone. "How are the girls?"

"They're fine. We found Zoe and Bella down the road a ways talking with a strange character in the backseat of an old rust bucket Ford station wagon straight out of the 1970s. It's bad enough he shouldn't hang out with teen girls, but more upsetting was his drugged condition."

"From pot? Alcohol?"

Tessa wrapped her arms around her middle. "Don't know. Though he was pretty wasted, there were no drugs or booze in sight. Folks always eyeball me as a user, but I've never tried a hit of anything but caffeine."

"That's two of us," Kierra said. "Finding the girls with this guy must have been scary. Do you think they got into his stuff?"

"They said no. And seemed pretty straight minded when we found them. But, who knows without a drug test, which I'm not looking to pursue."

"I can understand your concerns," Cami said.

"I'd be upset if that was my daughter." Kierra rubbed Tessa's shoulder, relieved her sister didn't withdraw from her touch. "Did you take the girls away from that charming young man?"

"Yes. With Zoe and Bella a wreck, and me upset, Mom offered to take them on a walk. I looked all over the place for you—I can use your company."

"I'm here for you."

Tessa wrapped a strand of hair around a finger. "The girls will never forgive us for interrupting their supposed fun time."

"Of course they will. You did what you had to do." Kierra turned to Cami. "As a mom and school director, what's your take?"

"Children—including teens—do come around when it comes to protection and love."

Kierra needed to tamp down on a flutter of nervousness and swallowed hard. She smiled softly at her sister. "You said there's a situation?"

Tessa scuffed her left orange sneaker in the sandy soil. "Well, I think so."

Kierra and Cami exchanged curious looks.

"What?" Kierra asked.

"Mom got the girls to calm down by starting their stroll singing at the top of their lungs. I'm nervous thinking that if they continue that loud way along the town's main drag there may be other troubles." Tessa smirked. "I know. It could be worse. But we're new in Kindred Lake."

"And you're concerned with what others think?" Kierra asked.

"Kind of. I wish Zoe were in my sight and wanting to talk with me. You know, on a daughter-to-mom level." Tessa sniffled. "What's the use? I'm an awful mother, and she knows it. I haven't been around for her and she doesn't want a thing to do with me."

That was exactly what Kierra and Tessa had agonized over their mom through the years, wishing Anna had a closer, more meaningful relationship with them. This was what Ryan experienced with his daughter. He too wondered if it was possible to win back Bella's love.

Kierra pulled Tessa into a hug. "I may not be a mom, but I understand what you're going through. As a family we need to know that the love we have for each other is reciprocal, given and returned freely."

"Zoe hates me. There's nothing I can do to make it better." A sob escaped from Tessa. "She's with Mom because grandmothers have a knack for painting the sky with rainbows and making flowers bloom through the snow."

"She'll be back," Cami patted Tessa's back. "And she won't want it any other way."

"Let's return to the inn," Kierra said. "You'll want to be there when they come home."

Tessa hiccupped. "Home. I love the sound of that word."

A mix of warmth and confusion swirled within Kierra. "It's a sweet word, indeed," she said softly.

With her sister upset, Kierra offered to drive them back. Thankfully, Tessa accepted. Five minutes later they pulled into the driveway.

"Looks like you have a visitor," Cami said. "Another guest checking in?'

"I'm not expecting anyone." Kierra did a double take. "Oh, that's Ryan's rental car."

"Thank God," Tessa said, as Zoe, Bella, and Anna climbed out from the vehicle.

Cami unbuckled her seatbelt. "Ryan, huh? And that's his daughter, Bella?"

A surprise zing buzzed in Kierra's chest. "Yes," she said as she watched Ryan slide out from the driver's seat.

"Doubly awesome. After we make sure everyone is safe and sound I insist you introduce me to uh...your..."

"Guest," Kierra supplied. And she was sticking to that safe, cordial relationship.

Tessa eyed Kierra. "What does that mean, sis? Never mind. I have a daughter to take care of." She ran to Zoe and without saying a word pulled her into an embrace.

Kierra grinned at Cami as she made her way to her side. "You're gaping at Ryan."

"You bet I am. Good thing I already have my beloved hunk and we're about to get hitched, otherwise I'd go after him."

Kierra smiled warmly at her friend. Cami had said what she said from an approval perspective, not as a jealous threat.

"On second thought, I'm going to take off," Cami said.

Kierra faced her friend. "I thought you wanted to meet Ryan?"

"Oh, I do. Another time, though." Cami's eyes became smiley with affection. "Enjoy, and I mean it." She headed toward her car.

"Thank you," Kierra called. Propelled by a force not her own, she hurried toward Ryan.

$\mathcal{T}$he last thing Ryan had expected from Kierra was her warm smile. Instead, maybe a cold shoulder or a frosty look of contention. Question after question, even. He deserved these for his abrupt departure en route back to the inn on their biking journey.

And he'd crossed the line of keeping a respectable and professional distance as an inn guest by kissing her. In that one little and agonizingly brief kiss he'd tasted a sweetness he'd nearly forgotten. Sweetness? Who was he kidding? That kiss awoke desires, not simply chaste feelings, he'd tamped down long ago when his marriage ended. What a kiss. Her lips against his left him wanting more. Much more.

Kierra exuded a sparkle as if she was the sunshine of daybreak, coloring the sky with peach, lilac, and orange.

Wow, he had it bad over her. He had to let go, as in she's off limits, buster.

Fat chance.

She glanced at the inn where the others had retreated then back at him. "Thanks for taking my mom and niece home."

"You're quite welcome. I was biking down Main Street and

came across the three of them. They might have been belting out a Broadway tune, but the girls' sad faces and your mom's worried look told me it wasn't quite the merry occasion."

"Did they make a fuss?"

"I asked them—half ordered and half begged, really—to stay put while I biked back to the inn to get my car. And here we are."

"Guess it was a good thing you chose the other route rather than continue with me." She rubbed at her arms. "For the record, that was said without sarcasm. Prayers for their safety were answered."

"Prayers, huh? I was also praying." He peered into her lovely eyes. "For everyone."

"Did the girls say anything in particular on the way back?"

"Zoe kept rubbing her teary eyes, saying she and Bella never touched the stash of drugs. As for my daughter, she seemed resolute in her agreement with Zoe, but also seemed shaken."

"Are you going after the druggie?"

"I've already contacted the police, and given his name and address, thanks to your mom. Told them this bozo was under the influence around minors." He glanced toward the road. "Sorry to bring the police to your inn, but there's the likelihood that they'll swing by."

"I understand. It's not a problem."

He let out a sigh of relief. "Thanks. I just want to get the girls settled down."

"May I make a suggestion?"

"Absolutely."

"Let's go inside," she said. "I have a few board games to keep us busy and hopefully in good spirits. The last thing Zoe and Bella need is to be alone and to overthink and worry."

"You're right. And I hope you'll be part of this *us*."

Her facial features went from a furrowed forehead to a soft smile. "I'd like that."

"I'm happy to hear that." Without another second speeding by, he grasped her hand. "No hard feeling between us?"

"Over...?" She touched his lips then fanned her fingers against her mouth. "Over what happened earlier? Over my self-imposed directive of keeping my personal life separate from my occupation?"

Swept away by her touch, he nodded. He'd have to rein in his self-control more.

"Do you think the girls would prefer Scrabble or Monopoly?" she asked.

"Let's go see."

*S*crabble won by a landslide.

As soon as Kierra served the tall glasses of icy lemonade, Team Bella and Team Zoe formed and manned the long sides of the table in the formal dining room. Team B consisted of Anna and Tessa helping Bella and Kierra and Ryan cheering along Zoe. The girls had chosen their teams and it made sense to everyone. With the competitive rounds of creative wording passing time and gleeful shouts filling the air, Kierra admitted to herself that she enjoyed working alongside Ryan.

Zoe placed two tiles around the letter u. "Mum."

Bella's eyes widened. "Hey, isn't that how they say mom in Britain? This is the US." She turned to Anna and Tessa. "Is that fair?"

They both nodded.

"Mum is a legit word," Tessa said. Her eyes turned glossy as she looked at her daughter on the opposite side of the table. "It has a wonderful meaning."

"Aw, Mom," Zoe said. "Don't go sappy on me."

Bella shrieked as she placed letters down on the board to

form the word *sappy*. She snickered like a cartoon villain. "Thank you!"

"Oh, keep quiet, girlfriend." Zoe stuck her tongue out at Bella. "You shut up."

"Girls," Tessa warned. "Be nice to each other."

"Yes, Mum," Zoe said with a grin on her face.

"Is anyone hungry?" Kierra asked. She had to get away from this mother-love conversation before her thoughts led her to a dark place, before her heart sagged, and her tomorrows once again appeared bleak. "I can make us a dunch."

"Is that somewhere between lunch and dinner?" Ryan rubbed his stomach with flourish. "I'm starved."

"Dad," Bella said. "You're always hungry."

Kierra started for the kitchen. "I have Gruyère and sharp cheddar for melted cheese sandwiches, homemade chicken noodle soup, and leftover..." She pivoted around halfway then stopped. She'd been about to offer Ryan meatloaf in case he was a meat and potatoes lover, but to her own betrayal, her eyes misted and a choke lodged in her throat. She dashed into the kitchen before she made a fool of herself.

Her mind might have ordered her to the refrigerator, but her feet took her to the sliding glass door in the rear of the kitchen. She pushed back the floor length yellow and green curtain that matched the room's interior colors, and leaned against the glass panel. Kindred Lake called out to her. Unlike her mom and sister she'd gladly forfeit excursions through shops selling items ranging from souvenir baubles to silk dresses. Give her the outdoors, beautiful nature full of color and sound and a pace of its own, and she was happy. In the open air she felt the closest to God she imagined humanly possible on this earthly side of the grave.

She rested her eyes shut and remembered another time outdoors.

A squirrel climbed down the tree beside their park bench.

"Quick Jonathan, give me the bag of walnuts."

He handed her the sack of animal treats, and a kiss.

Forgetting about the animal, she touched her lips. "What's that for?"

"You're radiant outdoors, and I love you."

"*A*re you okay?"

That wasn't Jonathan's voice. She opened her eyes. Ryan stood inches from her.

Relief swept through her from head to toe.

"I'm good." She turned away.

He placed his hands on her arms, both gently and firmly, and pulled her against his chest. She leaned into his hold, a good, safe place. Together, as a perfect fit, every knotted muscle from her temples to her toes eased.

Prepared for more questions, she waited. None came. She sensed he would be there for her for as long as she needed until she was ready to speak.

"Sorry. I'm usually not like this," she said, her lips moving against the soft fabric of his navy black and blue biking T-shirt.

"Like what? Real, honest, and coping like the rest of us, to the best of your ability?"

She peered into his warm, caring eyes. "You have a way of turning sad things bright."

"Funny, that's what I've been thinking of you."

"Honestly?"

"I never mince words."

With years of reporting on life as it occurred, he probably was as straightforward as they came. A good trait to have.

"That's a great view of the lake and hills," he said.

"Yes, I'm blessed." An arrow of self-pity shot through her. She groaned and turned toward the glass door, away from him.

He weaved his fingers through her hair, not letting her go. "You're upset. Is this about a once upon a time when you thought life would be different?"

Ryan got her. How? He barely knew her.

She faced him. "That's a definite understatement."

"I'm here for you." He stepped closer, mere inches separating them.

"I should be getting the food I offered. I shouldn't be thinking of myself. Shouldn't—"

"Emotions have a mind of their own." He pointed his thumb over his shoulder. "They'll be fine. They're girls and women. You know the drill, they're likely dancing the tangle of wanting to chow and fighting off the guilt of calories."

A giggle escaped from her mouth.

"That's better."

"Thanks," she murmured.

"I'm thinking that how you're feeling now is linked to Jonathan. Did you two ever marry?"

She blinked. "Oh, I'd forgotten I mentioned him to you."

"By name only. I can tell he's messed with you, though. And you're not over him."

She stared at her beloved hills on the other side of the lake. "It's not whether I'm over him than what could have been between the two of us." Laughter flowing from the dining room caught her attention. "What a lovely sound."

"Yes, it is."

A sob escaped her resolve to remain strong.

"It's all right."

"How can you say that?"

"Because Jonathan isn't with you. I am."

The cold of life drained from her; warmth seeped slowly and comfortably in. "I'm glad you're beside me."

He led her to the maple stools beside the kitchen island and pulled one out for her.

"I'm sorry I'm upset like this. On top of random thoughts of Jonathan, seeing my family, plus you and your daughter, seated around the dining room table undid me. The laughs. The friendly competition. The compassion and camaraderie between parent and child."

"Family."

She nodded.

"Which you want?"

She shrugged. "I thought that's what I wanted. I mean, yes, I cherish my mom, sister, and niece and although they're a handful at times, have welcomed them into my home...uh...inn."

"Then you're willing to chance your occupation and privacy for your family because you love them?"

"Yes."

"Commendable. And that's how it should be. Might you want more?"

She rubbed at her arms. "Meaning?"

"Your own child? For that matter, a good old-fashioned husband?"

"Jonathan and I had set a wedding date and..." She combed her fingers through her hair. "I thought I knew everything about him, thought we wanted the same things in life."

"Like children?"

She nodded. "I brought a gift over to him and was going to leave the surprise at his house to find after work. Instead, I found Jonathan sprawled across the couch, not looking so hot. He held a bag of ice..."

Ryan waited.

She sensed she could trust him. She met his eyes, determined to share despite the sensitive subject matter.

"We'd talked about children in our future. He seemed in favor. At least, he didn't rule it out. Well, Jonathan had just come back from the urologist. He'd had a little procedure."

"A vasectomy?"

"Yes," she said softly.

"It was that he didn't ask your thoughts about the procedure beforehand, more than the actual act, that came as a shock."

Not a question but a statement. Again, he was on the same wavelength as she.

"Yes." She wrapped her arms around her middle. "I could have been content with adoption. Also, I'd have been caring enough not to call the marriage off if he'd confessed that he couldn't conceive a baby. And who knows my reaction if from the get go of our relationship he'd been honest that he didn't want children? But, this? I didn't know what to do, how to react." She lingered around the real biggie then took a deep breath and let the raw truth out. "Then it became worse. My thoughts and feelings no longer mattered."

"What do you mean?'

"Because any options were taken away from me when he wanted the marriage called off. He said no kids, no marriage, and no commitment. Evidently, it took our approaching wedding day to make him realize this. Never mind what I thought, or wanted." Antsy, she pushed to her feet. "I ended up agreeing that things weren't working out for us. We mutually agreed to cancel the wedding." In need of fresh air she walked back to the sliding doors and pushed them open. She drifted to the deck's railing, giving her usually controlled mind the freedom to float away.

Nimble on his feet, she wasn't aware of Ryan approaching until he stood by her side. He covered her hand with his, his warmth an instant zing throughout her.

"A change of place and scenery will help both of us. Let's go grocery shopping for our dinner, the one I'll cook."

"But I have plenty of food." She pulled her hair into a ponytail then let it fall free to her shoulders. "Wait. Did you just say that you'd cook? For everyone?"

He nodded. "Are you game?"

"Most definitely."

He smiled, one that tickled her with unexpected joy.

"I'll go tell my mom and the others—"

"Let me make it easier." He backed toward the house. "I'll tell them where we're off to and bribe them with a promise of a scrumptious dessert for an exchange of no questions asked."

"Deal. My purse is hanging on the peg board to your right as you walk in, under my sweater, if you'd grab it for me."

He flashed her a thumbs up.

12

*A*s they weaved through the produce section, Kierra's attention divided between the fresh pineapples, the bright red vine-ripened tomatoes, and the six-foot dreamboat beside her, Ryan. She liked how easily they'd continued their conversation—a mix of both light and deep—from the car ride to the grocery store. She admired how he smelled the fruit and palmed the tomatoes for firmness. What she loved though was how he walked beside her as she pushed the cart, his attention, when not on food selection, fixed upon her. A spark lit his brown eyes giving him a sweet boyish excitement in a heavenly masculine mature body. Mmm, without a doubt.

They stopped before the bin of russets and white potatoes.

"Funny," she said. "We talked about nearly everything on the ride over except for dinner. Were you thinking meat and potatoes or chicken? The grill's set to go."

He brushed his fingertips over her hand. "I prefer working over a stovetop than grilling."

"A shame," she said in a carefree tone. "I'll have to introduce you to my barbecued smothered ribs and fresh corn on the cob."

"Well, babe," he said in a mock gangster tone. "You've got me hoping."

That worked both ways. About to tell him her feelings, the words lumped in her throat. Unsure why the twist in emotions, she returned to the safer subject of food. "Well then, what's on the menu?"

"To begin with, tossed salad with homemade dill dressing and toasted almonds. Then, how about old-fashioned meatloaf, crispy potato casserole with caramelized onions, and a side of stir-fried Brussels spouts and carrots?"

She gasped. "You're a foodie?"

He shrugged. "I'm fussy, like to eat, and find cooking fun."

"And your wife didn't appreciate that? Wow. I'd cling to you..." Heat torched her cheeks. She stared at the floor. "I'm sorry," she said softly. "My mouth sometimes gets ahead of my mind. That was wrong of me to say."

They strolled into the condiment and sauce aisle. He placed a bottle of ketchup into the cart, but remained quiet.

"Ryan, I'm sorry. I had no right to talk about your ex and you're probably upset with me. Want to leave? I'll understand."

He placed his foot on the cart's bottom shelf to stop her from wheeling further down the corridor. "Ketchup's the essential ingredient in meatloaf. Bet you didn't know that."

"Everyone loves ketchup."

He feathered his fingers over her cheek. "Your comment about Lisa isn't troubling. That marriage is over. Years ago. As I've already told you, I didn't throw in the towel; she did."

"You loved her?"

He gave a slow nod. "I love everyone that comes into my life. Each one is a gift from God to treasure." They walked toward the array of herbs and seasonings. "We began as a couple devoted to each other. Then things fell apart. I could have forgiven her romantic fling if a one-time stint, but...." He removed a jar of dill weed from the shelf then set it back and mumbled that he should go back to the produce section for fresh dill.

It was her turn to comfort him. She squeezed his shoulder. "But, she wanted out? Like Jonathan?"

"Yes." He faced her. "I believe in fighting to keep what is important in life, such as a marriage, but she didn't. I had no other options. Note this isn't a self-pity declaration."

"I hear you. Believe me, I do."

He smiled. "I know you understand, and I appreciate it. Appreciate you."

She glanced at the small list of items she'd scrawled during the car ride over to the supermarket. "I need paper towels and the never-have-enough TP. If you'd like, I'll give you the cart and you can go your way while I go mine and we'll meet at the front of the store."

"Actually, no." His lips twitched up, his smile irresistible. "It wouldn't be the same without you by my side."

Her heart pattered in a melodic rhythm. She scrunched the shopping list into her purse and gestured to the cart. "Lead on."

For the life of him, Ryan failed to understand the faulty connection between his brain, his mouth and legs when it came to Kierra. His mind warned him to cool it. He was an inn guest, what others might label as a free spirit. Sooner or later he'd pack his belongings and move on. Yet, his body, his whole being, refused to budge from her side whenever they were together.

Back in the inn's kitchen, he picked up the bottle of ketchup. About to pour a glob of the under-valued condiment into the mixing bowl containing ground beef, egg, panko breadcrumbs, oregano and garlic, his hand acted on its own volition and hovered over the food mixture as one specific word floated through his mind.

Dare.

Could he dare become attached to someone else?

He'd met, fell in love, and married Lisa and they had a baby girl they loved and cherished. And look at the mess he'd made of it since their divorce...the outcome being an emotionally detached daughter.

Could he dare, in the romantic sense, like Kierra? He'd come to Kindred Lake for the sake of Bella, wanting to desperately patch their relationship. What he didn't expect was to meet the gorgeous owner and operator of the town's sole bed and breakfast inn.

No. His daring days were over. His wasn't the Midas touch, but rather the Sadim touch. Sadim was the reverse spelling of Midas. The negative connotations were apropos when it came to him.

Bella's sweet laughter floated into the kitchen from the dining room.

He should leave Kindred Lake before he hurt his own daughter again. Once was enough.

"Looks like Scrabble is maxed out," Kierra said as she walked into the kitchen. "I can't keep the hungry savages at bay much longer. The nibbles of corn chips and salsa you've prepared were gone within minutes."

"I'll put the meatloaf in the oven and chop fresh salad right away."

She stepped to his side. "Says no man who stands with a bottle of ketchup over meat for a suspended amount of time." She gently lowered his hand to the island's white tiled surfaced. "What gives?"

As if she were the sun itself warming his back, her soft and tender voice helped to uncoil his knotted muscles. "Just thinking."

She lazily stroked the back of his hand. "Pondering often gets the best of folks a bit down in the blues."

"Would you like me to leave?"

"From the kitchen?"

"No. From the inn."

"Of course not." Her eyes widened. "Is that what you've been thinking about?"

He looked in the direction of the other room where his daughter, the love of his life, sat nestled in the safety and friendship of Kierra's family. "I'm concerned about interfering with your family and plans."

She brushed his cheek, her fingers scraping his five-o'clock shadow. She didn't pull away from the burn; he didn't step back from her touch.

He peered into her eyes, luscious in physical beauty, stunning in understanding and compassion.

"Is this about your wanting to leave?" she asked.

"Since you've expressed concern about reconciling with your family, I'm concerned about getting in your way. A little personal time, one without interference from a stranger as myself, might help."

She rubbed his back, her touch fast becoming addictive.

"I'm seeing things differently, Ryan. One, since your arrival, I've relaxed a whole lot more with my family than I ever imagined possible. Two, you have this way of uniting all of us, including your daughter. By the way, did you realize that while you're slaving away in the kitchen, you're missing out on totally unexpected fun out in the other room?"

"Is there a number three?"

"Yes. And, three, I like you. A lot." A smile lit her face. "There. I said it aloud."

"Do you have misgivings?"

"Not one."

He pulled her closer, breathing in her sweet scent of floral blossoms.

A chant came from the dining room. "Feed us...feed us...feed us..."

Hesitant to separate, he trailed his hand down her back. She leaned against his chest. Their gazes locked, and they remained that way. Staring at, inhaling in, listening to every hitch of breath, all of what made the other person. What felt like both hours later, they pulled apart.

As she raked her hand through her thick brown hair, his desire grew to weave his fingers through the strands, to fan his fingertips across her cheeks then to her mouth where he'd press his lips upon hers for an indefinite time.

He groaned when the food chant increased in volume. "Can you soothe the hungry gang while I prepare the salad?"

"Can do," she said. She took a couple of steps then glanced over her shoulder and gave him a dazzling smile. "I'll tell them about our post-dinner plans."

"Post-dinner what?" he said. Too late. She'd left the room. He laughed so hard he clutched his middle. That woman knew how to make him buzz with joy. Curious to know what their new plans were he quickened his pace of food prep, the sudden distance between them multiplying by the mile.

$\mathcal{K}$ierra grasped Ryan's hand as they strolled along the hilltop's grassy surface. "Never underestimate the fortitude or timing of a woman."

"Or, a woman's excellent planning strategy." He spun her around to have a view of her family and Bella, below. "This after-dinner walk was a great idea."

"Thanks." She pointed at her sister sneaking up behind Zoe and Bella. With arms extended, Tessa was poised to grab them. "Oh oh."

Ryan's lips swooshed to the right in amusement. "Tessa is going to scare the daylights out of them."

"No she won't. Watch."

Both Zoe and Bella whipped around and screamed silly at Tessa. Tessa whooped in surprise. The girls burst out in laughter and started to roll on the grass as if putting out a blaze.

"I'm going to get you two knuckleheads," Tessa shouted in obvious playfulness. She wiggled her fingers. "You better run."

"No way, Mom," Zoe shouted. "I'm not afraid of you."

Scary grunts came from behind them.

"My mother to the rescue?" Kierra mumbled to Ryan as Anna

joined Tessa in the ranks of monster terror and marched toward them. Quick to their feet, the girls ran. Anna and Tessa gave chase.

"I never thought the girls would fall for the suggestion of hunting..." She gasped as he ran his fingertips, soft and slowly, up her bare forearm. She swallowed hard. "Of hunting fireflies this time of year."

Sirens filled the air.

Ryan flinched.

Below, Anna, Tessa, and the girls stopped and quieted.

"Oh, dear. That's the fire whistle," Kierra said. "Kindred Lake's ace volunteer fire department seems to be getting more calls lately. I hope it's not someone's home or business."

"Or accident," he said softly.

She remembered what he'd revealed about Maryland's Back Alley Fires, how it cost a life, homes, businesses, and to this day, ongoing heartache. She patted his arm. Hope was essential to share and foster in others. She didn't want him to be shaken when the roar of fire trucks screamed down the road. "The fire house is close by so don't be surprised by the noise."

He nodded and pointed to the girls as they launched into a dance routine. "Look at them go. Nothing stops them. They're like a couple of adorable puppies running off excessive energy after chow time. Praise God they're happy."

She searched his face for clues for surfacing old hurts. He appeared at ease and she was relieved for him. More trills of mirth came from below and she saw her mom and sister jumping into the dance fray. "Yes, praise God for all good things."

He tugged her hand downward and they sat on the grass.

She drew her knees to her chest; thankful he was there with her. "You seem more relaxed."

"Than when you found me in the kitchen meditating with the ketchup?"

She shrugged. "Hey, if ketchup works, I won't come between the two of you."

He laughed. She loved how light his normally deep speaking voice rose each time a hearty chuckle escaped his alluring, charming lips.

"I was stuck in my thoughts. About family, work, and assorted reluctances."

She cupped an ear. "If you want to share, I'm listening."

"Fear controls many of one's choices."

"Yes, that's right. Anything else?"

He flashed a grin. "That will have to wait for another time."

"I can respect that," she said, though he'd piqued her curiosity. Since ending her relationship with Jonathan her senses had slumbered in a deep sleep, but upon meeting Ryan she'd come alive. Yet, she wanted to give him as much personal space as he needed. "Seriously though, you don't have to share a thing with me if you don't want to."

"Thanks." He waved his hand before them as if pushing away a pesky fly. "Enough about me. Despite Jonathan, you've managed to move beyond fear." He glanced behind them at the direction of the inn. "You're a sole proprietor of your own B&B. Pretty gutsy."

"Gutsy, huh? I don't think of myself that way."

"Oh, you are. And committed to what matters to you. I sensed that when we first met."

She grinned. "When you first arrived at the inn, my family was moving in and my nerves were a mess. It's amazing I didn't send you scurrying down a bike path away from this town, let alone me."

"The moment your niece called out that your mom and sister were tangled in the next world war, it was obvious who mattered the most to you."

"By leaving you, a paying customer, and attending to my family before business?"

"Exactly why."

"That's gutsy?"

"Yes. Quite a few awful social situations have shown me how others are more concerned about moneymaking opportunities than family." He reclined back onto the grass and patted the empty space to his left and waited for her to settle alongside him. "Were you always this way?"

She pressed down on her lip as denial and truth battled within her. Memories, both happy and sad, stirred her as she settled beside Ryan, a place she wanted to be more and more. "To be honest, no. I love my mom and sis, and niece. Growing up though, it was every female for herself." She shivered despite the 60-something degree spring temperature. He inched closer and pressed into her side. Again she shook, but this time with the sudden feel-good hum from his proximity.

He grasped her hand. "Tell me."

Should she share about when her mom decided to make her food blog into a career and left her and Tessa to practically fend for themselves until she'd found Anna hunched over her keyboard in the middle of the night and demanded equal time with her *competition*? About the time she talked her sis out of running away from home with her boyfriend? Ah. She had the perfect zany tale. "Do you like vampire stories?"

He propped on an elbow. Their enveloped hands dropped between them, close to their hearts. She inhaled a whiff of peppermint on his breath.

"Love them."

"When little, I tumbled into a valley of fear each time I heard the word needle. On one humid July afternoon, my mom had an eye exam. Tessa was at a friend's and Mom insisted I, at age eight, should not remain home by my lonesome, and I tagged along. The doctor, who enjoyed greeting his patients, stepped into the waiting room and called Mom's name. When we both looked up the doc's bushy brows lifted and he said that it looked like he had two patients, not one."

"He had an eye for things."

Kierra smirked. "Bad pun."

"I tried."

And that he did. She appreciated how he always tried to lift her spirits. She hoped she did the same for him.

"What did the doctor say was wrong?" Ryan asked.

"Oh, nothing that a good surgery to tighten weak eye muscles couldn't resolve."

"And the needle part?"

"Back then, the thought of doctors ripping into my eye sockets didn't rate high on the worry charts. I'd seen a few movies when, post-surgery, the handsome physician strolled into the patient's hospital room and smiled warmly at the person tucked comfortably in bed. The patient always returned the doctor's smile, and that was enough to convince me that surgery and recuperation weren't a big deal. What troubled me were the blood-sucking vampires Tessa conjured up. You know, the ones that did the pre-op testing. They'd surely stalk me and drain my arms of blood."

"Anna didn't put a stop to your sister's stories?"

"Mom said not to worry, that after the vampires got enough blood, they'd leave me alone to rest." She paused to allow the past to exit from the present. "In hindsight, while Tessa may have been a tad on the obnoxious older sister side, Mom had tried to calm my fretting over the surgery by abetting Tessa's story, thinking it was comical enough that I'd laugh over the matter rather than wanting to hide under the bedcovers the rest of my life."

Ryan lifted a brow. "And you know this about your mom how?"

"I confronted Mom, a little later than I should have. But we had a good talk."

"Excellent. You're way ahead of others learning to deal with fears at a young age. How did the embracing family part come into play?"

"That's the lesson I never thought eye surgery would have provided." She slipped her hand free from his hold and sat up, again hugging her knees. He sat up as well, his hip touching hers. She didn't inch away.

"The same procedure I had is far different today," she continued. "Back when I was a child they kept me in the hospital for three days. Although I wasn't in a private room, the bed next to me was empty. I'd drifted off to sleep during the long night, when suddenly two nurses barreled into the room. This was it, I thought. The vampires had arrived. Turned out the nurses wheeled me into the room next door. They needed my room for a medical isolation case."

"That must have been scary."

"It was, but my fear of never seeing my family again replaced my fear of vampires. See, I'd been convinced that Mom and Tessa would never find me. The nurses said they'd inform Mom of where I was, but I wasn't buying it. I cried so hard I'm surprised they could operate the next morning."

"Ah, it was the eternal separation from your family that concerned you then?"

She eyed her mom and sis and the two girls as they chased each other below the hill. As if Anna sensed Kierra's contemplation, she stopped and peered at her. She waved, motioning for them to come down from the hilltop and join them. Kierra smiled. With this handsome, caring man beside her, and of her loving family close by, warmth filled her from head to toe.

"Yes. Oh, we squabbled lots during the ensuing years. Actually, right to the time Mom and Tessa came to live with me. I opened the door for them, and they entered, so to speak. Slowly but surely, things are changing for the better."

She didn't realize he'd again reached for her hand until he placed her fingers against his lips and kissed them, one by one.

Sweet shivers, like the kind one gets from listening to the comforting chime from a breeze rocking a mobile of seashells, spread across her arms.

"You are a beautiful woman," he said, his voice thick and husky.

14

*L*ike the old jokes about the chicken that crossed the road, as Kierra climbed the rocky incline, she wondered whether she'd ever look back upon this time and crack the joke about why the washed-up chick braved a hiking trail by herself, the one clearly marked Caution. With her mom and sis in town browsing antique shops, and Bella's mom busy, Ryan and she invited Bella and Zoe on a hike. After last evening's lovely firefly outing, the girls readily accepted, making for a perfect Sunday afternoon.

Now, after making a pit stop, Kierra rushed toward the direction she'd last seen the girls and Ryan. They'd all vanished faster than a magician's rabbit.

She cupped the sides of her mouth. "Hey, guys. Where are you?"

"Aunt Kierra," Zoe called. "We're here."

Kierra shielded her eyes from the sun streaking through the trees and painting an already picturesque area more breathtaking. She had to admit, with Ryan's presence, the wooded area looked pretty amazing. Make that gorgeous.

"Nice to see everyone again," she said as she approached the threesome. Zoe, kneeling at the base of a tree, pointed to a creek. On the opposite side sat Bella crossed-legged. She hurled pebbles off the water's surface. Ryan, squatting a few feet to his daughter's left, also skipped rocks across the flowing water.

Kierra pushed back brush and made her way toward Zoe. She knelt beside her niece. "Have either said a word?"

"Nope," Zoe replied, her voice shaky. "Bella started to get freaky. Aunt Kierra, she's moody. She's tough one moment, and wobbly the next. I can't read her. I'm worried. Will she be okay?"

The answer Zoe wanted eluded Kierra, but she couldn't tell her niece, the child who cared about each person to the point of physically aching for them, that she has no idea for certain. "Bella needs time, and space. But, with you as her good friend, and her dad beside her in love and support, she'll come around. You watch."

"I'm not a good friend."

"Oh, sweetie, why do you say that? Of course you are."

Zoe kept an eye on Bella as she responded. "A good friend sees this kind of stuff before it happens and tries to make it cool again."

Kierra clasped Zoe's hand. "The most important thing a friend can do is to be there for the person. You, my love, are definitely there for her." After a few beats of silence she added, "Bella is a strong person. And sometimes, headstrong is advantageous."

"And other times?"

A tough question. A tough world they lived in.

"Bella and her father have several issues to iron out that's likely upsetting her."

Zoe's eyes flashed wide. "But it can be straightened out, right? I mean, it's not like it's permanently bad?"

"Of course. Your friend has a lot going for her, especially with her dad's love and support from the rest of us."

"Hey, look, Aunt Kierra. Ryan is signaling for us to come over."

Kierra glanced across the creek. Her breath caught. Warmth spread throughout her. Bella, tucked under her father's protective arms, wore a contented expression.

Hand in hand, Kierra and Zoe stepped on rocks and crossed the creek.

"Hey you two," Kierra said.

"Hey yourself," Bella replied, sans a bite.

Ryan ribbed his daughter playfully in the side. "Hey," he said, his voice deep and playful.

"Hey," Bella repeated.

Zoe squatted at Bella's right. "Hey," she muttered, then giggled.

Bella again chirped the word, followed by Ryan.

Kierra, with hands on her hips, shook her head in exaggeration. "You guys sound like a bunch of croaking frogs."

"Hey," Ryan said and patted the ground beside him.

Without delay, Kierra plopped down. As Ryan extended an arm around her, she also croaked her own *hey*.

Before them the creek's trickling water carried away the remaining tension, nature's version of a maternal hush. The sounds of a buzzing bee and a crow's caw helped push away the din of the passing train miles away, its echo always heard throughout Kindred Lake. Kierra couldn't remember a more precious moment.

Ryan peeked at his watch and leaned toward Kierra's ear. "It's half past two. Let's say we head home."

Home? He could have used the word *inn* or generalized it by saying *let's go back*. Instead, he said *home*. Had he meant that? She hoped so. Hoped he was comfortable in Kindred Lake, at home...with her.

She nodded, not daring to utter a word to disturb the peace

besides the babbling creek running through these bright green and lush woods thickening by the day with a new spring. Heading home, with Ryan and the girls, sounded better than the loveliest symphony she'd ever heard. Only good awaited them.

15

_T_he beauty and tranquility Ryan had experienced a mere twenty minutes ago proved too good to last. Two police cruisers awaited them at the inn. Parked on the curve of the driveway, the vehicles reminded him of bloodhounds sniffing out trouble.

Infernos of out of control fires leaping from house to house, business to business, flashed before his eyes...

Fear tightened the emotional noose around the necks of gathering onlookers.

A child went missing, then tragically found.

To push the past away, Ryan gripped the steering wheel hard. His palms burned. A tender hand covered his. He glanced to his right.

"Whatever this is about, we'll handle together," Kierra said.

"Dad?" Bella said from the back seat. "What's happening?"

Focus. He loved his daughter. He cared for Zoe. And although it defied his sensibilities, he was downright smitten with Kierra. Wait a second. This scored more than simple attraction. His dreams told him that. He had to protect this woman and the girls.

"God's with us," Kierra murmured.

She was right, of course. He turned around to face Bella and Zoe. "Don't worry, we'll be fine. Why don't you and Kierra stay in the car and I'll find out what's up with the police?"

Before they could reply he slipped out of the vehicle. Three doors slammed behind him. So much for the gals remaining in the car. As he approached the officers, Tessa and Anna trotted down the front porch steps.

"They just got here," Tessa called.

"Can I help you, officers?" Ryan asked.

Kierra stepped forward. "Hi, HoJo," she greeted the older cop. She tossed a hello-Ben to the younger one.

Ryan toggled his attention between the cops and Kierra. Right. Small town. Everyone truly did know each other on a first-name basis. For better or worse.

HoJo, a probable nickname. Likely, he'd enjoyed many stacks of pancakes from the once popular Howard Johnson's restaurant chain. The silvery-haired officer offered Kierra a faint smile as he ignored the others. His gray eyes the shade of gloom, added to the quickly mounting tension. "I'm afraid this is strictly a business call."

Kierra clutched the V of her red tee. "I can't imagine why."

Officer Ben studied Anna and the girls. He withdrew a writing pad from his shirt pocket; his pen poised over the paper, ready for action.

Ryan stepped back and put an arm around Bella and Zoe. He must have pulled them to his sides tight because they both flinched.

HoJo pursed his lips. "Might be a good idea for the girls to go indoors."

Bella crossed her arms. "I'm no kid. I'm staying."

Zoe smirked as she eyed her mom then the officers in defiance. "If she's staying, I'm staying."

HoJo lifted his chin toward Ryan. "And you are?"

"Ryan Delaney."

"A guest at *my* inn," Kierra said, her emphasis loud and clear. "It's not every day that you two pay a visit. Please, no more suspense. What's wrong?"

"Is Anna Madden your mother?"

"I'm right here." Anna hooked arms with Kierra. "Please talk to me directly."

HoJo glanced at the girls then zoomed his attention onto Anna. "Ms. Madden, you accompanied Bella Delaney and Zoe Madden downtown—"

"Excuse me, officers," Anna said. "I know Bella, and Zoe is my granddaughter. No need to address us as if we're a bunch of criminals."

Both officers lifted their left brow in unison.

Ryan's jaw dropped. What kind of nonsense was this?

"Hold on, there." Kierra fanned her arms out.

With her shoulders slung back, head high, and fists clenched, she stood in pure defense mode of the ones she loved. In Ryan's eyes she couldn't be any prettier.

"My family recently moved in with me, from Massachusetts," Kierra added. "I repeat, they're family. In case you don't get that, I'll spell it out for you. Anna is my beautiful mother. Tessa is my beautiful sister. Her daughter, Zoe, is my beautiful niece. And Bella Delaney is a beautiful friend. The only time my mom and the girls walked about downtown Kindred Lake was when Mom wanted to cheer them up." She paused, though her breath wasn't choppy nor did she appear unnerved. "The last I knew, singing in public isn't against the law. They certainly weren't breaking the town's noise ordinance. Don't scare us." She hooked gazes with Ryan. "And don't think twice about this good, decent person that I've had the blessing of getting to know."

HoJo returned his attention to Anna. "Ms. Madden, do you recall throwing away a piece of paper into a trash receptacle?"

"What are you getting at?" Tessa started to shake her finger at

HoJo and didn't stop when he asked her to. "Is singing plus throwing away trash illegal in this town?"

Anna seized Tessa's hand. She looked at both her daughters then at Ryan. "Yes, I recall distinctly emptying my pocket of unwanted junk. Know why?" She gave the officers time to reply but their silence prompted her on. "Both Zoe and Bella were upset, in tears if you must know details. And while I was at it, I also scooped up and disposed of a few discarded papers next to a trashcan."

Zoe covered her face with her hands. Bella ducked her head against Ryan's side like she used to do when she was three and terribly shy.

"My granddaughter," Anna continued, "and her friend had just experienced a traumatic and frightening encounter with a lowlife drug user. That boy is the one you need to go after and hound with questions, not me. Nor the girls." She swept her gaze around to the rest of her family, and at Ryan.

Something wasn't adding up and Ryan had to jump in. "Officers, what was found in the trashcan that's troublesome?"

Both cops looked toward the inn then back.

Bella pulled back from Ryan's side. "Are we going to be arrested, Daddy?"

He couldn't remember the last time his daughter called him daddy. He shook, not in fear but rage over how these cops terrified everyone. He bent to whisper in Bella's ear. "I love you, sweetheart. I'll make sure we're okay."

Bella gave a little nod.

"A town camera caught you discarding paper." HoJo cleared his throat. Again, he eyeballed Anna. "While it's legal to throw away trash, what is suspicious is the threat written on the note."

Both Anna and Tessa opened their mouths but HoJo sliced the air with his hand. "Ladies, you must permit me to talk." He waited in silence to test them, but when they failed to speak he rewarded them with a testy smirk. "That's better. There have been a few suspicious fires in town lately."

Beside Ryan, Bella gulped audibly. He placed a hand on her shoulders; he'd ask her later about her reaction. He reined in his focus on HoJo, the pancake lover.

"One of the papers you disposed of was a note similar to the ones we've found about town, and in a similar scrawl." He turned to his partner. "Ben, tell them what the note stated."

Ben referred to his notepad. "Be careful. You may be next."

"And what else was found on the note?" HoJo asked.

"A doodle. A brick chimney with smoke wisps gushing out into the air. It's sketched in pencil, but the smoke is heavily blackened and smudged."

Ryan's insides choked. Once again, he smelled the fires of destruction.

16

*T*he moonless night suited Kierra fine. Perched on the top step of the inn's back deck, the afternoon's events kept replaying in her mind. What began as a delightful hike in the woods with Ryan and the girls hit a blip when Bella turned gloomy, but Ryan jumped to the rescue. For a dad estranged from his daughter, he knew exactly how to pull her from the dumps. Croaking like frogs, who would have thought? If it not for his love of Bella, and wanting to make her happy, Kierra doubted they would have enjoyed the afternoon. Ryan was a good person. Then, they arrived back to the inn where the police greeted them.

"What's going to happen, Aunt Kierra?" Zoe said from behind her.

Kierra glanced over her shoulder. Her niece leaned against the outside door. She looked lonely, afraid, and helplessly young.

"Come sit beside me," Kierra said.

Zoe slid beside her. "So?"

Wary from the day's topsy-turvy events, Kierra rubbed her eyes. "I don't know, sweetie. I believe Grandma when she said she'd picked trash from the street and then disposed of it in the garbage can. That's just like my mom. She's always detested litterbugs. I also believe you and Bella had nothing to do with the fires."

"Do you think Ryan's behind the fires?"

"I know Ryan well enough to say that there's no way he's setting the fires." Images of the Back Ally Fires, tangled with Ryan's troubled face when he'd mentioned the subject, convinced her he was no fires starter. "The intense way Ryan loves others spells clearly he'd never hurt anyone."

"Like my mom loves me? Like how you and Grandma love me?"

Kierra nodded. Before her family arrived in Kindred Lake she'd questioned the strength of love they'd had for each other. In just a few weeks she'd experienced love blossoming anew between her and her mom and sis and onto the next generation between her niece and new friend.

And, between her and Ryan?

Love. A true possibility.

"Yes, dear Zoe. Exactly that type of love. Good, kind love."

Zoe yawned into her shoulder.

"Tired?"

"I'm totally beat." Zoe pecked Kierra's forehead with a wet, sloppy but sweet kiss. "Good night, Auntie."

Kierra smiled as her niece took off to her room.

She jumped at the swooshing sound of footsteps coming from the shrubbery below, but then steadied herself as Ryan appeared at ground level.

"Mind if I join you?"

"Please." Before he'd left to take his daughter back to her mom's he'd changed into a long sleeved plain white shirt to fight against the approach of the chilling night air. Beside her and spotlighted by the back light, the white shirt set off his short-cut black hair, tanned and healthy-looking features from being outdoors, and his boyish smile that had surely charmed many a female TV watcher.

With his presence, she was no longer cold from the evening air. "How are you tonight?"

He stood and stretched a hand to help her onto her feet. "I'm beat from the day's events, but too wired to sleep. Come with me for a walk and we'll talk more."

*R*yan stuffed his clammy hands into his tan chinos, the one pair of slacks he'd purchased in addition to the two pairs of jeans upon arriving in Kindred Lake. His heart thumped an extra beat against his ribs. A chuckle escaped his lips.

"What?" Kierra gave him a sideways grin.

"You have this way of making me...well...um..."

"Tongue-tied?"

His chuckle morphed into a sputtering laugh. "Yeah," he said when he calmed down. "What I wanted to say was young."

"You're not ancient."

"It's been years since I've felt this alive, and it's all your doing."

She reached for his hand. "That's better," she said as they entwined their fingers. "I was hoping HoJo and Ben's visit didn't killjoy the day for you."

The cops' little investigation annoyed him and vexed his patience, but he could deal with those two. "The one thing that nearly undid me today was seeing Bella upset."

"Teens, especially teenage girls, are awfully moody. Chalk it off to hormones or the challenge of exerting confidence while feeling totally inadequate." She let out a half groan, half chuckle. "Extends right into womanhood."

"Guys go through this as well. We just don't admit it."

"I'm sorry Bella is troubled. It's good timing that both she and Zoe met each other when they did. A good friend goes a long way."

"Definitely." They entered a lakeside park full of gardens and he made a mental note to take Kierra back during the daylight. Together they could enjoy what must be riots of reds, purple, and pink spring blossoms opening to the sunlight. "I still wonder whether she's over the breakup of my marriage to her mom."

"Everyone has their own recovery rate from surprise."

"How well I know that truth."

She tugged his hand and pointed to a bench. "Want to sit and talk? Otherwise, we're about to exit the park and I'd like to prolong this time together."

What he wanted to do was to pull her against his chest, kiss her, and forget about the rest of the world. For now, he'd settle with her suggestion. "Lead and I'll follow."

"Ha. Not every man I meet says those words."

"Every man, as in men? Good thing I know your teasing."

"Am I?" Without waiting for his response, she ushered him toward the bench and they sat. Not one inch separated them. "Tell me, how are you coping with those two bozos' accusations? I've known HoJo for a long time. His partner, Ben, is new on the force and I'm not as familiar with him, but he seems nice. I've never questioned their police tactics until today. A whole different light beamed on those two and it wasn't pretty. The nerve of them pointing their suspicious fingers at my mom. I can't believe..." She quirked her tempting lips upward. "Wait a second. Why are you smiling?"

"Because of you. This afternoon, when we encountered those cops at your place, you made me admire you more."

"Admire," she repeated, her word sailing on a floaty breath. "How?"

"By the way you defended your family. From what you've shared with me, before they came to town they teetered toward hopelessness. With your loving influence, I see your family becoming a tighter knot, how it should be. Plus, you've included Bella and me." He patted his heart. "That means a lot."

"I sincerely meant it. I'm glad you and your daughter have come into my life. I'm glad you're not simply an inn guest passing through town."

He eased closer to her mouth.

She pressed her palm against his chest. "Have you...and Bella...ever talked about the fires in Baltimore? May this growing fire concern in Kindred Lake be upsetting her?"

"We've talked a lot. Back when the Baltimore fires happened, and subsequently when I took a leave of absence from work she was more nervous for my sake. You're right, though. These random town fires seemed to have struck a sensitive chord in her. She's confided in me that she could never torch a place and make others suffer. I believe my daughter."

"I also believe her."

He leaned toward her. "Let's put aside this topic."

"Want to continue on our walk?"

"No." He cupped her face and covered her lips with his. He saw bright colors and felt the firm dimensions of beauty and the sharp angles of strength. He tasted her, pure goodness.

17

"*A*unt Kierra?"

The digital clock on the oven had just flashed to twenty minutes past midnight. Kierra pushed aside her untouched chamomile tea that she'd brewed in hope of falling asleep. A futile attempt since she didn't want to sleep, not when she could sit under the soft kitchen light hanging over the table while thoughts of how scrumptious Ryan's lips felt upon her own played over and over in her mind.

"Hey, Auntie…"

Kierra faced her niece who wore pink jammies and an orange robe. She was glad Zoe chose brighter colors these past few days and hoped the trend would continue. "What's up?"

Zoe scrunched her nose. "I've never seen you so spacey. I tried calling to you a second ago, but I guess you didn't hear me."

The word *sorry* nearly slipped from her mouth, but tired of apologizing for herself, Kierra held back. "Here you go." She pulled out the oak chair beside her and patted the seat. "It's reserved for you. Come join me."

Zoe slipped onto the chair. A yawn exploded her face. "'Cuse me. I'm crazy pooped, but can't sleep."

"That makes two of us." Earlier she'd spoken with Ryan about his daughter and the impact of the officers' visit, but they hadn't mentioned her niece. "Why can't you sleep?"

Zoe shrugged. "Because."

She pulled the pale-faced teen closer and gave her a kiss on the cheek.

Zoe rubbed her face. "What's that for?"

"'Cause I love you."

"I love you too." Zoe rolled the upper right corner of her placemat. "Bella and I were texting each other. You know, about what happened this afternoon with the police."

Kierra nodded, but remained silent. She wanted her niece to make the next move.

"We got talking about lots of things." Zoe flattened the placemat then began to roll it again. "Like about her dad. You know he was a big reporter on the evening news where he lives, right?"

"An award-winning news anchor." She grinned. "I Googled it after he told me a little."

Zoe slapped her a high-five. "Way to go."

"Ryan may return to the news station."

"Bella says he's on a sort of leave from the place." Zoe worried her bottom lip. "She also told me about those horrible fires. And the little girl who was...killed...because Ryan couldn't save her in time."

"Oh, honey, he tried his best. He feels horrible that the child died."

Zoe sniffled. "That's sad."

"Yes, it is. In my eyes, though, Ryan is a hero for trying to rescue her. He could have been killed as well."

"I said the same thing to Bella."

"What was her reaction?"

"She texted a shrug emoji."

Kierra had told Ryan that, like him, she believed Bella

wouldn't start a fire intentionally, yet she was curious about her niece's take on her friend. "What do you think about Bella and her reaction about these strange fires happening?"

"She's worried about her dad. She doesn't want him to get upset again."

"It's good that she's concerned about Ryan. He's strong, kind, and brave." She'd never considered another man in those descriptive terms, not even Jonathan.

"Do you like Ryan?"

She wasn't quite comfortable responding to her thirteen-year-old niece about whether or not she liked Ryan. Besides, another question burned her tongue. There wasn't any other way to paint her next question in pretty pastel colors, so she pushed it out before she went chicken. "What about the time you and Bella called 911 about the trashcan fire by the library?"

Zoe jerked away. "Why? Do you think she'd start a fire?"

"No. And I told her dad as well. But I do know that sometimes people start fires to get attention."

"She wouldn't do that, Aunt Kierra. I know her. She's not mean." Zoe glanced at the beige pressed tin ceiling then glanced back at her. "Like I had said, she was more into the firemen who showed up."

"Firemen?" Tessa said. She plodded into the kitchen, her slippers slapping the floor. "Did they show up and no one woke me up for the party?"

Both Kierra and Zoe stared at each other then grinned.

Without waiting for an invitation, Tessa sat at the table. She rubbed at her eyes. "Well, since I've joined Team Insomnia and know there's no going back to bed for me, is there a lousy cup of coffee in this place?"

Kierra stood. "No, but I'll brew you a great cup of coffee."

The side glass door slid open. Ryan, in the same biking attire he wore when he'd arrived in Kindred Lake, stepped indoors. "Coffee? I'd love a mug or two."

All eyes riveted onto Ryan. He wore skin-tight clothing that made him look more panther-like than human. Kierra did not want to pull her attention away, but the ever-wanting-to-please inn hostess kicked into gear. "Coffee coming in a snap." She hurried to the drip coffee maker to put up a full pot.

"Couldn't sleep either?" she asked over her shoulder.

"Didn't try," he said. "I know myself when I get things on my mind."

Were you thinking about me, she wanted to ask. She couldn't stop thinking about him either. Didn't want to stop.

"I hopped on my bike and went to the same park..."

She raised a brow to hopefully prevent him from revealing more in front of her sister and niece. She'd never escape Tessa's teasing and Zoe's questionable glances.

He studied her expression and scrunched his forehead. "...the park with those blossoming cherry trees."

Kierra opted to play it safe. "You should see that park during the day. Pure beauty."

"Yes, I imagine."

From the corner of her eye she caught her sister's wide-eyed look. "Tessa, call me sleep-deprived, but I'm drawing a blank. How do you take your coffee?"

"Black, like Ryan's biking duds."

She'd have to rib her sister later how she noticed what Ryan was wearing in the middle of the night. For now, she'd play hostess. She knew of one way to control roaming attention spans: Food. "To go along with the coffees, I have lemon cake and apple pie. Both are home baked. What would everyone enjoy?"

Tess and Zoe chose the pie and Ryan the lemon cake. She too favored lemony tastes, another similarity they had in common. He was becoming more and more larger in her life by the second. She sliced big hunks of the cake, no guilt, and placed two servings of the pie, also large, in the microwave.

"Delicious," Ryan mumbled minutes later around a mouthful of cake.

Zoe forked another bite of pie. "Hey Aunt Kierra, tell us about the lemonade girls. Ever since I saw that photo of you and Mom I've been curious. Mom and Grandma won't talk about that summer."

Kierra and Tessa exchanged glances.

Tessa shrugged. "Why not?"

As she had experienced when she shared about the lemonade summer with Ryan, Kierra again inhaled the aroma of tart squeezed lemons, felt the trickle of sticky juice on her forearms, and tasted the sugar they used to sweeten the fresh beverage. She remembered swatting away pesky flies, making small talk with customers, and sharing jokes with her sister. Most of all, she could...

She blinked back tears.

Ryan placed a hand on her shoulder. Not caring about what her sister or niece thought, she didn't inch away.

"Did something bad happen then?" Zoe asked.

Kierra swiped at her eyes. "Just the opposite."

Zoe glanced at her mom, the need for support obvious in her eyes.

"Only good stuff," Tessa agreed. "We kept each other company that summer."

"What's special about that?"

Kierra managed a little smile. "For us, Zoe, it was unusual. Your grandmother suggested the whole biz about selling lemonade because she didn't want us to get bored and drift into trouble. We didn't fight, didn't scream at each other; it was like an enchanted spell was cast over us. You know that saying about making lemonade from sour lemons?"

"Nope."

Tessa reached for Zoe's hand. "You take the upsetting parts of life and make it sweet and delicious."

Zoe studied the connection of her and her mom's hand. "Like today? Like we can take what happened with the police earlier and make it into a good thing?"

"We'll make it work positively for us," Kierra said. She looked into Ryan's eyes. "Plus, as Ryan's been reminding me, by including God in our lives and asking Him to help us, we can get through rough times and greet brighter tomorrows."

"Amen," Ryan said.

"Kierra, sweetheart," Anna called from the kitchen's entry. She leaned against the doorjamb and rubbed at her belly. "Cake and pie?"

"I thought you were on a no-sugar diet, Mom," Tessa said.

Anna stared longingly at Tessa's last bit of pie. "I can say that too about you, but I won't. At times, sugar is a necessary bliss."

Kierra motioned at the vacant chair beside her. "Come on over and add your own wonderful, lovin' sugar."

Anna, halfway toward the table, stopped. She ran her fingers through her sleep-ruffled hair. "Kierra? Did you just pay me a compliment?"

Kierra drifted back to summers ago when the sweetness of lemonade and summer and family lightened each step of hers, setting free the forgotten joys of what love could be like between a mother and her daughters year round.

That happiness became evasive, escaping their reach when she and Tessa began the new school year in September and Anna again buried herself in her work. The three of them slipped into the same old routine of tension like it had prior to the summer. She began to doubt that enjoying each other's time during those golden days of July and August had been a wild daydream and not reality.

Could they ever share that love again?

Mom wasn't getting younger, nor was she. Only one answer existed.

Warmth spread within Kierra. "Yes, Mom. I meant what I said.

You've been loving and sweet. Before I get weepy again and embarrass myself, would you like a slice of lemon cake or apple pie?"

"Oh, thank you for the kind words," Anna said softly. "I'd enjoy a slice of cake, like that gentleman is wolfing down." Anna winked at Kierra. "That man beside you has excellent taste."

18

*A*lthough Ryan was considered in the biking world as a fast roadie, he wasn't a racer. The fastest speed he'd clocked riding his bike on a flat surface was 20 mph. At that speed he'd had a physical and mental workout. He'd trained months to achieve that velocity plus the focus it demanded. He couldn't beat that sense of accomplishment on any level, including when he was at his peak career-wise as an award-winning news anchor. But this thing happening between him and Kierra had grounded him silly. He couldn't move, fast or slow, without her by his side.

Then, there was his daughter to consider. Bella was the reason why he'd come to Kindred Lake. He couldn't push her aside to shower his attention on a woman. Didn't want to.

A woman?

Kierra wasn't a blend-in-a-crowd woman. She stood out. She called out, to him.

A car door slammed shut and jabbed at his thoughts. He glanced up from the front porch rocker toward the inn's driveway in time to see Bella wave goodbye to her mom as she drove off.

"Hey, Dad. You look serious. Are you sure about me hanging out with you today?"

"Without a doubt. I always enjoy spending time with you." Perceptive as always, Bella was right about his overloaded mind but he didn't want to go there with his daughter.

She scuffed up the walk, hands stuffed in her front jeans pockets. Since she'd been hanging around Zoe there was no longer the stench of cigarette wafting from her clothes and hair. He'd wondered how he could influence her to quit the nasty habit, but thankfully her new friend had intervened.

"Is Zoe around?"

He glanced at his watch. "Inside. She's a late sleeper, but she might be awake now."

"I guess seven in the morning is early for a Saturday. What do you want to do? Since I'm done with my homework, it could be a whole day thing. Can Zoe and Kierra come along?"

Kierra. Was she brightening his daughter's world as much as she'd brought the sunshine back into his own life?

"Aww, you'd like my company," Kierra said from behind them. She greeted them with a wide smile. "Good morning, lovelies. Anyone for eggs and toast?"

Before his mind could toss out objections, Ryan stood and hitched his thumb toward the door. "Let's go in."

The three of them followed the aroma of fresh brewed coffee into the dining room where Tessa, Anna, and a sleepy-eyed Zoe sat around the table. Two empty chairs begged them to join the smiling crowd.

"I've been waiting for you," Kierra whispered into his ear.

The joke-telling competition at the table grew fierce and funnier. When the two teams formed, Ryan and Tessa verses the girls, Kierra had bowed out due to hostess obligations. She couldn't guess who would win. Her mom, the judge, kept score of the knee-slappers or groaners, a good thing since her attention swirled around Ryan's every forkful of egg or sausage, sip of black coffee, and crunch of toast.

Tessa poked her side. "Are you going to answer the phone or want me to? Sounds like your voicemail is on strike."

"I'll get it." Kierra excused herself, catching the observing eyes of her sis and mom. She hadn't been aware of the incoming call.

She thought her friend Cami would be on the other end to arrange a time to meet again. Instead, Jake Kinkaid, Cami's fiancé's father, greeted her with a hearty hello.

"Good morning, Mr. Kinkaid. How may I help you?"

"If you have time today, I'd like to pay you a visit."

"I'll be happy to meet with you." She listened as Jake excitedly shared his news. They agreed that in one hour, before either Cami or Gavin might catch wind of what Jake had in mind, he and his wife would drop by.

"See you soon," Kierra said. Wow. She wasn't expecting that.

"I didn't know it was possible," Anna said, "but you're smiling from head to toe. What gives?"

Kierra slipped back into her chair beside Ryan. She rubbed her arms, more jazzed by joy than chilled. "This is so beautiful." She paused to stifle tears.

"Oh, brother," Tessa said, the josh in her tone both thick and sweet. "She's going to bawl like a baby."

Ryan patted Kierra's hand while grinning at Tessa. "I'm here for you...even if your sister isn't."

Anna squealed. Tessa snorted. Both girls rolled their eyes as if to silently agree that the adults at the table were either sappy or silly or both.

"Tell us," Ryan said. "Investigation's in my blood. I have to know."

Kierra sniffled. "Let me tell you how Cami and Gavin came to the point of falling in love and wanting to marry. You'll have to know a little about their past that dates back to their school days and—"

"Childhood sweethearts, how lovely," Anna said.

"No, Mom. I'm afraid that wasn't quite the chemistry those two shared." Kierra looked at her niece then Bella, and took a chance without consulting Ryan that her friends' story was permissible to be heard by teen ears. "Those two were actually enemies, on the bitter level. Cami, and a bunch of other kids, bullied Gavin and his family."

"Sad," Tessa said and gave Zoe a hug.

"It is." Kierra admired her sister's growing tenderness and sensitivity since she'd moved in. Tessa was trying extra hard to offer support to her daughter, to everyone. "And it's alarming how often bullying occurs." She weighed her next words with care. "Cami and Gavin fell in love and forgave each other of their past wrongdoings." She searched for the right words. When her gaze darted straight toward Ryan, she knew the way to convey the tangled story. "But, their families crept between them. Don't get me wrong. Cami loves her family, and Gavin his."

"Then what's the problem, Aunt Kierra?" Zoe set her fork down. "Sounds like one big love-fest to me."

"As their relationship grew, they managed to right things first with Cami's folks. Gavin's dad was a whole different story since back when Gavin was a teenager he'd made his son vow not to have a thing to do with Cami as an adult."

"And the resolution was...?" Ryan prompted.

Kierra smiled softly at him, "To confront family kindly and bring God and His loving help into the picture."

Ryan's brows lifted, his forehead wrinkled. "What happened?"

"Let's just say that Jake Kinkaid and his wife are coming over because they have a huge surprise for his son and future daughter-in-law." Kierra heard the sparkle in her tone and let out a full-octane squeal of glee. "They're going to prepay for the entire wedding ceremony, which will be a total surprise and blessing because Cami and Gavin have no idea Jake and his wife had saved through the years for their son's hopeful wedding. Jake loves Cami and says he wants to further welcome her into the family with open, unconditional arms by doing this little for them."

"Little?" Anna said. "That's a lot, both love wise and financial wise."

"Sweet." Tessa plucked her napkin from the table and wiped at her eyes. "This is making me cry happy tears."

Ryan pushed away from his place setting. "Ladies, after the Kinkaids visit, we need to celebrate this inspiring story of love and commitment. It's a great day to go bike riding." His eyes twinkled at Kierra. "I suggest we circle around the lake. I understand it's a special lake where love and harmony are rediscovered."

Kierra set her coffee mug onto the table. "Oh? Where did you hear this?"

"I've been learning a lot since I've been here."

"But, Dad," Bella said. "Only you and Kierra have bikes."

"Yeah," Zoe added. "If you want to consider Aunt Kierra's as a legit bike."

Kierra faked a pitiful sigh. "Thanks."

"Girls." Ryan crossed his arms. "What am I ever going to do with you two?"

"Huh?" they said in unison.

"I've already befriended the owner of the bicycle shop on Madison Street and—"

"Oh, right," Bella said. "He rents out bikes. Wished I thought of that before I opened my idiot mouth." She dropped her chin, but not fast enough to mask the disappointment.

Ryan bounded right to his daughter's side. "Sweetheart, you're intelligent and awesome." He bent over her chair and draped his arms around her. "Your teachers think the same about you and marvel about your great grades."

"Well, they are improving." A tiny smile lifted the corners of Bella's lips. "Like a lot of things around here."

ive females followed Ryan as they biked alongside Kindred Lake. With the steady drum beat of happy chatter, the occasional strike of the cymbal of amazement as they passed by a particular scenic view of countryside, and the surprise trombone slide to announce one of the lovely ladies catching up to him, he felt like a grand marshal of a parade. He glanced over his shoulder at Kierra behind him, her ponytail lifted in the breeze. Her niece, side by side with his daughter, followed. Kierra's mom and sister brought up the rear riding on a shared yellow quadricycle with its red and white striped canopied roof and black seat for two. He'd logged hundreds of miles, possibly into the thousands at this point, in long-distance biking, but never experienced an endorphin rush to this degree like this moment.

Blessed.

Yeah, that was more like it. No way could he rightly chalk this no worries moment off to mere coincidence. It had to be orchestrated by God.

"I think the troops are hankering for lunch," Kierra called.

He slowed his pace to give her a chance to catch up. "After

that breakfast? You kept bringing out fresh from the oven blueberry muffins and that was on top of the eggs and toast we'd already enjoyed."

"With that huge smile stamped on your face I'm doubting that was a true hardship."

He pushed his hands off the handlebars, straightened, and rubbed his gut. "You have that right. Just glad I'm working it off."

"Tell me about it. My metabolism isn't what it used to be back in my prime."

"Prime, as in a thing of the past?" he said. "You're beautiful."

A flush tinged her cheeks pink. "But everything has a zenith point before it's a steady downhill."

"Nope. Some people—specifically you—are beautiful no matter the age or condition."

"You hardly know me."

He winked. "I know what I see."

A flat, tired honk came from behind. Ryan glanced over his shoulders to see Bella and Zoe nearly upon them; identical grins stretched their faces silly.

"Hurry, you two," Bella shouted. "We're about to invade your private lovey-dovey talk."

"Is that what you think we're talking about?" Kierra said.

"Ha," Zoe chimed in. "You old dudes can't fool us."

Kierra pumped harder to add distance between her and the girls. Ryan did the same.

"Hey," Zoe called. "Are you like, what, secret athletes?"

Kierra laughed and began to pass Ryan, but he caught up. He was glad to have her to himself again. "You're wonderful. Kierra, believe me, I never toss out an insincere compliment."

"You always say what you mean?"

"I do, honey."

Another toneless honk came from behind.

They laughed as they heard shouts of wait-up.

*W*hile Ryan kept the girls busy at one of the picnic tables alongside the lake with tales of past bicycle tours, Kierra and her sis and mom emptied the two picnic baskets from the quadricycle.

Anna stroked the bike's canopy as if a cherished pet. "I might just save my pennies for one of these fun bikes for two. It's always the right time to meet a good man." She sighed dreamily. "Of course, you two could borrow it for special occasions."

"Mom," Tessa said, fingers pressed between her eyes. "What are you implying?

Anna swept a motherly look from Tessa then Kierra. "You know, darlings, this world is a scary place at times. I just want the best for you. I'd hate to see you both linger in loneliness."

Part of Kierra wanted to accept her mom's gentle words at face value. Anna had softened a great deal since she arrived in Kindred Lake. Gone were her self-centered ways and harsh judgment. However, there was this...meddling of sorts.

Oh, stop, she scolded herself. Mothers love. They care. They want the best for their children. Didn't she just say those exact words?

A full reconciliation between each family member might finally show and stay if she and Tessa put down their guard against their mom. They needed to accept her as a Mother with a capital M. A mother who meant well.

Kierra watched a small squirrel climb down a tree and guessed it was a baby old enough to leave its nest for an adventure. She hoped its mom was watching out for it. She looked at her own mom. "Go on, please."

Anna's attention strayed to Ryan busy pantomiming some sort of critter and making the girls laugh. "Knowing you're loved, and giving that love back, does take the sting out of life."

Kierra's eyes brimmed with stinging tears. She did an about-face from her mom and sis.

Two hands pressed and squeezed her shoulders.

"I meant to be hopeful and encouraging about brighter tomorrows," Anna murmured. "I didn't mean any reflection upon you and Jonathan. I'm sorry if I upset you, honey."

"I love you," Tessa said.

Kierra closed her eyes to absorb the warmth offered from her precious ones flanking her sides in support and love. Slowly, she nodded. "I know. It hurts, though."

"I imagine it does," Anna said.

Kierra opened her eyes and faced her mother. "Mom, when did you get over missing Dad?"

Anna smiled softly. "I never have. And it only hurt more when he passed on afterwards."

"Wow. To think you were already divorced by then." Tessa placed her free hand on their mom's shoulder while holding onto Kierra.

"That's right. Realize though, I forgave your father for wanting out of our marriage. Then I was able to let go."

Lines creased Tessa's forehead. "Wait a second. If you forgive and let go of someone, how could you still miss him?"

Anna shrugged. "Emotions can be a beast. They rear their ugly heads at times and take control. I don't understand, but it's like you mourn the things that might have happened in life but didn't because of another's abrupt departure, whether divorce or death."

Kierra inched away from them enough to wrap her arms around her middle. "That's exactly it. Jonathan's gone. Like it or not, he's out of my life. But, those thoughts...daydreams of what might have happened encircle me like a lasso."

Tessa glanced at Zoe, still a ways away, then back at Kierra. "Like the children you might have had?"

"Or the anticipation of arriving home after work or errands to the one and only stability in your life?" Anna added.

"Yes, both." To her own ears, Kierra's reply was but a mere swish of air. "And more."

Anna unwrapped Kierra's self-embrace and pulled her into a hug. Her mom remained silent, but that was fine. She needed her love and warmth more than words and that was exactly what Anna offered.

Beats of seconds...or minutes...slipped by. Kierra sensed her mom's attention had strayed and turned to see Ryan with the girls. Companionable chatter filled the air, though the distance made it questionable to know what was being said. The three of them seemed at ease with each other and most of all, happy.

"Sweetie," Anna said. She waited until Kierra faced her before she continued. "How about if you gather Ryan and the girls and tell them lunch is ready?"

"That's a fabulous suggestion, Mom," Tessa said. "And I'll help with the food."

"But we have everything done," Kierra said. "Why don't—"

"Sweetheart, listen to your wise mother." Anna winked. "Sometimes, she may offer a pearl of good advice."

*A*nna reached over the picnic table and offered Ryan the green and blue striped bowl of chicken noodle salad with ginger dressing. "More?"

"No, thanks." Between Anna's contribution of the salad and rollup sandwiches of turkey, goat cheese, and cranberry mayo, Kierra's peach pie bars and chocolate mousse cupcakes, and Tessa's family-size bag of potato chips, everyone either rubbed their full tummies or sighed in content. "I've already devoured two helpings. Anna, I might bachelor it up in the kitchen, but I'm going to check out your food blog and become a subscriber."

"Mom does an excellent job." Tessa gestured toward her sister as if a game show hostess showcasing the jackpot prize. "But, my sister's talent in the home department would have me coming back year after year if I were a paying inn guest."

Seated opposite of Kierra at the picnic table, Ryan nodded. "For sure."

"Thanks, sis," Kierra said. "Since I run a bed and breakfast inn, I better have this so-called skill you're talking about."

"Oh, please." Tessa rolled her eyes. "That's not a skill like throwing a dart and always hitting the bullseye. Creativity is a gift from God."

Kierra smiled. "I'm happy to hear you acknowledging God."

Memories of Ryan's own parents and extended family flashed before him, followed by the first few happy years with Lisa and Bella. It had been a long time since a group of people had made him feel accepted like these women did. Group? No, make that kin, in the true sense of family.

"Well, I've done a lot of thinking since arriving in town." Two lines appeared between Tessa's brows. "Just maybe there's more to us coming here."

Kierra rested her arms on the table. "What do you mean?"

"We could have checked into other apartment rentals, but then you called." Tessa's eyes widened. "Let's face it, sis. You have to admit our relationship had been strained when you welcomed us into your home."

"Tessa, do you realize you used the past tense when referring to our relationship?"

"I do. Let's keep it that way."

"I want to. You're my only sister and you mean the world to me. The bumps of life sneak between family members easily enough and disrupt. I get that." Kierra smiled. "Together, we can move forward. That's what counts."

"Exactly," Tessa said. "And that's why I'm trying to honor God because it can't be simply coincidence that we've come together again. Not after a few years of...of..."

"Tension and bad feelings?" Anna suggested.

Both Kierra and Tessa nodded.

Ryan grasped Bella's hand. She reached for Zoe's. One by one, around the table, they connected with interlocking firm grips.

"Dad, are you about to pray?" Bella asked.

He nodded and led them in a prayer of thanksgiving for family healing and new beginnings. A chorus of amens circled about the table. He pulled his daughter into a tight hug. She didn't squirm away. He had her back in his life.

Nothing would separate them.

20

*K*ierra felt a little tap to her foot. Instinctively, she peered across the picnic table rather than at her feet. Ryan smiled as if he'd heard a weather report forecasting a year's worth of seventy-degree perfect biking weather.

He wiggled a finger back and forth between them. "Want to take a walk?" he mouthed.

Fast on her feet, she couldn't wait. She loved her family, loved how the two girls were becoming fierce friends, but could use a bit of quiet. Serenity was more her speed and she believed Ryan not only understood that about her but embraced it as well.

"Hey," Anna called. Where are you two—"

Kierra spun on her heels to cut her mom off from possibly saying *lovebirds*. Those kisses they shared indicated clearly that she and Ryan liked each other. Yet, neither of them had professed love for the other. Until they did, she didn't want anyone pushing relationship pressures on them.

"We're taking a walk, Mom." She glanced at Kindred Lake. "After being cooped indoors all winter, I can't get enough fresh air."

"And my skin gets crawly unless I'm outside," Ryan said.

Bella laughed. "You get crawly if you have to hold still for two minutes."

Ryan shrugged his right shoulder. "What can I say? Some of us are blessed with energy and ambition."

"Ooooh," Tessa and Anna chorused.

"You know what you're in for now, don't you, Ryan?" Zoe said.

He nodded. "Yep. Unmerciful razzing from my darling—and when's the last time I said beautiful and sweet—daughter."

Kierra hooked Ryan around the elbow and tugged him along. Happily, he didn't resist.

Halfway toward the water, away from listening ears, she broke the silence between them. "I'm glad you asked me to join you for this walk. I've been needing a little space from them."

"I sensed that." He took a big sidestep to his right. "Although if space is what you need, I can appreciate it. I'll hightail it elsewhere."

She pulled him closer to her side. "Don't get any ideas, mister. You beside me is exactly what I want and need."

He gaped at her then rubbed at his mouth, but not enough to cover the right corner of his sweet lips twitching upward.

"Spill it," she said with a clear tease in her tone.

"I have to tell you that you made my heart pound by saying you need me beside you. No other woman has ever said those words to me. I actually couldn't speak for a few seconds."

They stopped walking. He lifted her hand to his lips for a kiss. When his mouth swept across her bare ring finger tingles sparked within her.

"And my words made you feel how, exactly?" she murmured.

He led her to the walking path that circled the lake. He then surprised her by a tug into a copse of willow trees.

She loved willows and looked upward at the branches that were yellowing in blossom. She pointed upward. "Here's hoping the tree's promise of shade is a sign of good things to come."

"Oh, I believe it is." He leaned toward her, moving closer and closer to her mouth.

With difficulty, she pushed him away gently. "First, answer my question."

His lips spread thin in a serious look. "Lady, I'm so swept away by your beauty that I can't recall what you asked."

She wrapped her arms around his neck. "How did you feel when I told you I wanted you beside me?"

"Like a boy on his first date with the girl he'd thought would never go out with him."

"Wow. I did that to you?"

"And more." He leaned closer, his lips again near hers. "You made me feel as if I wore scuzzy jeans and you, in a Cinderella gown, asked me to waltz with you around the moonlit garden." He cupped her face.

"You're a romantic."

He groaned, and they tasted again the sweetness each offered.

In no rush to finish their kiss, she'd lost track of time. For once, her super organized and over-scheduled self didn't care.

He pulled away first. "Since I'm unsure how long our privacy will last, let's continue on our walk."

"Sounds good."

Hand in hand they strolled another five minutes, the silence between them comfortable. Robins flitted about and sung to their mates only to be drowned out by the sweet sound of a gaggle of toddlers playing with toys as their moms watched and chatted away.

"I'm thinking about you and your daughter," she said in hope he wanted to talk.

"Yes?"

"I've observed you and Bella becoming closer. It seems like she's relaxed a good deal."

"I believe she has. Since coming to town I've been trying my hardest to give her the attention she needs. I know I can't make up for the past, but together we can move forward."

"Every child needs a loving parent." Kierra looked at the lake. "What about when you go back to Baltimore? Are you...I mean... do you think you can...?"

"Return to anchoring the news? Leave my daughter behind once again in the name of making a career for myself?"

Afraid of his answer, but wanting the best for him and Bella, nervousness engulfed her. "Yes," she said softly.

"The one thing I counted on during my biking trip to Kindred Lake was leaving the past behind. But, I wasn't expecting other changes."

She stroked his arm. "Oh?"

"I'm unsure if it's something or me that's different. Since coming here, meeting you, re-bonding with Bella, and honestly, chatting with God more than ever, I've been feeling steadier on my feet."

It was her turn to swallow hard. "Do you think you can again speak publicly, reporting the news?" *Miles away from her.*

"Yes."

She closed her eyes.

A kiss alighted on her forehead, the touch gentle and beautiful like a butterfly.

"The real question is, do I want to?"

She opened her eyes. "Do you?"

"No. I came to Kindred Lake to look after my growing-way-too-fast child. I want her to know she has a father in her corner to lean on. As for work, I'm done with fame, done with focusing on bad news for the sake of high ratings."

"I think that's wise. A good family has always been important, but these days it seems that as the world spins quicker and out of control, family is a treasure that shouldn't be relinquished." She nudged the begging question lingering in her mouth. "And us?"

"I'm for seeing what happens." He frowned. "Sorry. That came out wrong. I'm for *making* it work for us. I like you, Kierra."

Like. Not love.

First Jonathan, then Ryan. What was it about her falling for noncommittal men?

To be fair, they needed more time together. They hadn't known each other that long. It was early May, and he'd arrived here only three weeks ago.

"I like you as well, Ryan." Her words left a disappointing taste on her tongue.

"Great." He smiled. "Want to head back to the gals?"

"Sure."

As they strolled down the path they heard giggling in nearby bushes and stopped, surprised when Zoe spoke.

"It's kind of awesome."

"You think?" Bella said. "It wasn't your dad kissing some woman."

"Kierra isn't just *some* woman, she's my cool aunt. You gotta admit that it's nice to see them fall in love. Don't you want your dad to be happy?"

"What about the ick factor?"

"Oh, stop."

The girls broke out in more giggles.

"Are you going to tell him?" Zoe asked.

"About my mom's decision?"

Beside Kierra, Ryan tensed.

"Yeah, Bella," Zoe said, emphasizing the word *yeah* in two syllables of amazement. "About moving."

"I guess I'll have to. Mom and Alex are getting married this July. They're already looking at places in Colorado to be near his family."

"Wow. That's like a whole country away. I'll miss you."

"I'll be totally lost without you." Seconds ticked by. "But I don't know about telling Dad. He's trying real hard to patch things between us. Once we move I'll never get to see him."

"You will on school breaks and summer vacations."

"Who counts that? It's like he'll stop being a dad again. He'll probably go back to Baltimore, blab away on the news, get people to pay attention to him, and forget about me. It happened before, and it will happen again. You watch. I'm right."

"Maybe you'll be split between them. Like, half the time you're with your mom then half with your dad?"

"Right. Part-time parents. Part-time family. Big whoop."

"Hey, at least you have a dad. He cares about you. Not like me."

"Is that your cell phone buzzing?"

"Probably Mom's texting." Silence. "Yep, that's her. They want us back. Let's go."

The rustling of brush and scuffing footsteps followed.

Kierra turned to face Ryan, but blinked. He was gone.

She looked at the direction they'd just come and saw him walking slowly, more like dragging the weight of his soul.

"Ryan?" she called. "Wait up."

Without turning around, he continued on.

21

*A*s if acting on cue when Kierra returned alone from her walk with Ryan, the sun ducked behind heavy gray clouds. When the barrage of questions shot her way from her mom and sis about what happened, and whether they should wait for Ryan to return or try to beat the rain and bike back, her mood also turned gloomy and matched the sudden change in weather. She'd tried to explain Ryan's absence off to receiving sudden unexpected news that he needed time and space to think about. She couldn't help notice the exchange of curious expressions between Zoe and Bella. She wasn't going to fill in the details, though. She had enough on her own mind to ponder.

They agreed to head home. The girls took the lead followed by Anna and Tessa pedaling their shared bike for two, and Kierra last.

Last. She was growing to detest that word.

She was tired of always being last. Last to know Jonathan had opted to have a vasectomy, ultimately changing their life choices. Last to know Mom and Tessa and Zoe needed a new place to live. And this...whatever *this* was of Ryan's reaction to and handling the secondhand big news about his daughter's likely move miles and miles away from him. And this after riding on a high of believing their relationship was deepening.

"Holding up back there?" Tessa shouted over her shoulder. "We'll almost home."

Home.

"Acing it," she said.

"Totally not buying that. Good thing you're not in the sales business or you'd be broke."

She knew her sister. Tessa's tease rode bareback on a snicker, half in a sisterly taunt, half in an attempted humor to pull her out of the blues. She slowed her pace and slipped further behind from her family.

Ryan had said he didn't want to return to the news station. He was finished grabbing attention with sad, horrific stories. Instead, he'd wanted to brighten his daughter's world. Commendable. Still in the throes of patching the fragile connections in her own family, that made Ryan a true hero in her estimate.

Yet. And wasn't there always a yet? What about the two of them? She wasn't the type to push aside her morals and integrity to chase after passion, yet Ryan hadn't been in town that long before she'd given in to his kisses, responding to her attraction over him. So strong was this pull toward him that it seemed as if no other possibility existed.

I'm for making it work for us. From his sweet lips to her happy ears, he'd said those words,

I like you, Kierra. He'd also said those words as well, without a mention of love.

Perhaps a loving relationship like she imagined, like she longed for, wasn't meant to grow between them. He might be the type who wanted to only cozy up with her for a night or two in her bedroom. She couldn't imagine that, though. Had she misread Ryan Delaney one hundred percent?

The girls, her mom and sister, swung right onto Kindred Lake Inn's white-pebbled driveway. Kierra followed then stopped when she saw the vehicle she'd never expected to see again parked before her doorway.

*H*e held the bouquet of long-stemmed red roses as if seeking protection with a shield. Was he half expecting missiles to launch against him?

Little bursts of stars exploded before Kierra's eyes. With pools of sweat trickling down her back, she dug her toes deeper into the driveway pebbles in hope of resisting the dizziness. "Why are you here?"

Jonathan smiled and lifted the flowers a few inches. "They're make-up roses."

She let his words swim around in her mind and take root, but they failed to have meaning. He might have had the same sandy-hair, big and bright hazel eyes, a winsome smile and the fine chiseled features that lured her to him in the first place, but he hadn't changed at all. He also now had a rough edge about him, a look of power and possibly the audacity to use it. She saw it in his squared-back shoulders, the slight tilt to his head, the spread-apart feet ready to pounce if necessary.

"It's over between us, Jonathan." Relief spread throughout her when her mom and sister stepped beside her in support.

Zoe crossed her arms and frowned. "Is that the bozo that dumped you when you were about to get hitched?"

Jonathan lowered the bouquet. "Listen, I don't know you, kid. But this isn't a concern of yours. And besides, that's not what happened with us."

"Are you saying it's none of my business?" Zoe smirked. "I love my aunt and care tons about what happens to her."

Kierra hated to see her niece caught in a sandstorm that needn't happen in the first place. "Zoe, sweetie, I appreciate you defending me, but Jonathan's right. He didn't dump me. We mutually agreed to call the wedding off."

"He definitely dumped you," Tessa said. "The moment he stepped into that doctor's office and stopped thinking about you and your dreams in life was the day he dumped you like a garbage can dragged to the road on trash day."

Kierra should have known that if anyone would become fiery, it would have been her sister. She eyed Tessa in an attempt to signal that this wasn't the type of conversation to have within the range of teen ears. On the other hand, did it matter? They'd called off the wedding, the rest of their lives together. The end.

She peered into Tessa's eyes. "Sis, can you and Mom take the girls inside?" She jutted her chin toward the door in emphasis.

"But—"

"Please, Tessa."

Tessa's jaw dropped, but she and Anna corralled the girls with the bribe of making smores. Kierrra wished she could gobble copious amounts of chocolate and melted marshmallows, anything but face the former fiancé she hadn't bargained on confronting again.

Jonathan waited until Kierra and he had the outdoors to themselves before he narrowed the distance between them. "It's been a long two years. You're looking pretty wonderful."

Jonathan's big-eyed look of a hopeful boy, paired with the pursed mouth of a seductive man, flustered her more. She wanted to both cry and laugh.

He thrust the bouquet forward. "They're only flowers. I don't mean harm."

She kept her hands to her sides. "They're red roses. You know they symbolize love. They convey deep emotions."

A smile lifted the corners of his mouth. "There you go. I do have deep emotions for you. Always have."

"I'm sorry, Jonathan. I no longer have them for you."

"Aw, come on, lovey."

At his use of the once affectionate pet term for her, she stepped back.

He stepped forward. "We haven't talked fully about things before calling off the wedding."

Like her sister, her mouth went slack-jawed. In need to push words out before he could say more, she rubbed away at the shock. "We certainly completed everything necessary to say. We came to a mutual acceptance that it was over between us. Please leave."

He tightened his hold on the roses and winced. Had a thorn pricked his palm? "You need to let go of what happened and grab onto what waits ahead."

"What's the purpose of this conversation?" She tucked a strand of hair behind an ear. She wanted to remain pleasant, but her blood heated. "Has no other woman wanted a thing to do with you and you're crawling back to me?"

He clucked an uncharacteristic tsk tsk. His whole aggressive mannerism seemed out of place for the person she once knew. She clutched her collar and again stepped backwards. He followed. What was this awful dance they shared?

"I haven't hauled one insult at you, lovey...what's gotten into you? Why this change?" He narrowed his eyes. "This ugly side doesn't suit you."

She opened her mouth to argue but stopped when he scrubbed his face with his one free hand.

"I didn't mean that. What I'm trying to say is that we can advance our relationship as the Mr. and Mrs. that obviously we're meant to be."

The only thing obvious was the true blessing that they'd called off the wedding. Chills shot down her arms. Her instincts told her to run, but her mind reminded her that she wasn't one to flee a difficult circumstance. Besides, this was her home and place of business, her property. This was Jonathan, not a serial killer. Despite his odd persistent way, he meant no harm. Right?

People change. Sometimes for the worst. Right?

She glanced toward the inn.

"They're inside," he said. "Forget them." With the roses he pointed at his car; one loose stem fell to the ground. "Let's go for a ride. We'll grab a cup of coffee and talk."

"I don't think that's a hot idea."

He smirked. "Well, I could mention a few others hot ideas... and we'll talk afterwards."

Was this Jonathan? He surely wasn't the person she once loved and wanted to marry.

She pivoted around to face the road in time to see a bicyclist zoom toward them.

$\mathcal{T}$he one life lesson Ryan learned from reporting the news was to always expect the unexpected. When he saw a stranger stepping toward Kierra as she retreated further back, he jumped off his bike and ran to her, reaching the pair within seconds.

"Kierra?" he called. "May I help?"

A look of relief spread across her face.

The stranger's brows slanted inward. "Hey, there."

Whoever he was, he needed acting lessons on charm.

"And you are?" Ryan asked.

"I can ask the same, buddy." He smirked. "My fiancé and I were hashing out a few things. We'd appreciate a bit of privacy."

"No, *we* wouldn't," Kierra said. "I can speak for myself, Jonathan. And, I will—we're no longer engaged. Leave, now."

"Oh, Jonathan, huh?" Ryan placed a hand on his shoulder, pleased that Jonathan stiffened. "I've heard about you. Nothing pretty."

Jonathan dropped the bouquet, the cheap green gas-mart cellophane unwrapping as it fell. The flowers splayed in an uneven puddle. He ground them into the pebbled driveway as he stepped toward Kierra.

Ryan pushed Kierra to the side then placed his hand again on Jonathan's shoulder. "Hold it right there. Listen to her and put your sorry self into your car and hightail it away."

"And one reason I should listen to you?"

"Trust me," Ryan said. "You wouldn't want to find out."

Kierra started to stab the keypad on her cell phone. "I'm calling the cops."

"Move away from my sister," Tessa shouted as she sprinted toward them. "I've phoned the police. They're on their way."

Jonathan stepped back, both palms lifted. "All this fuss over me?" He glanced at Kierra. "Me, the person you were about to marry?"

"We're finished." Kierra's voice carried over the blaring sirens as the police approached. "Take off, and I won't press charges."

Jonathan took a few strides then stopped and faced them. "This isn't the end. We'll talk more, and that's a promise. I'll make you remember why I'm worthy of becoming your one and forever husband." After a cold stare he grinned. "You have no other option, lovey."

This clown was a classic piece of bad work. Ryan gave chase, each muscle rigid with disgust. Out of the corner of his eye he caught Tessa doing the same.

With the clumsiness of a jittery confused animal, Jonathan scampered toward his car and jumped behind the wheel. Without a word more he proceeded down the one side of the drive as the police cruiser sped up the other end. Tessa ran into the house, most likely to assemble the troops.

Ryan hurried over and embraced Kierra. He hated the way she trembled within his hold. "How are you holding up?"

"As best as can be."

"I'll see to it that jerk won't hurt you."

She cringed.

Alarm bells sounded in his brain. "You said it was over between you two...did I overreact?"

"No. Thank you for stepping in. Definitely on the heroic side."

He eyed the two cops approaching, thankful they weren't HoJo and his partner. "Why did you promise not to press charges?"

"The idea of slamming a person I once loved with a formal complaint is unnerving. Besides, he's hot air. I know Jonathan, know that he'll leave me alone."

Sadly, Ryan knew those were often the last words many exes exclaimed while alive. "I think you should hit him over the head with charges."

"This advice from someone who took off when he overheard bad news?" She lifted a brow. "I care about you. I want to help you through your troubles, not watch you walk away from me, like other guys I've known and fell for. And yes, that does imply I have this thing for you, Ryan Delaney."

Relief. She'd fallen for him. He pulled her tighter against his chest. "Sorry. I'd just heard, indirectly, the awful news about my daughter relocating miles away from me. I reacted in shock. I admit, it may not have been the best way to handle things."

"You needed time alone to think."

"Yes."

"I can appreciate that." She tilted her head upward, her chin scraping against his shirt. "How I reacted just now may not have been the greatest way either."

He wanted her around. He may not have known her for long, but he liked everything about her and easily imagined the two of them hitting it off further. About to tell her, the officers hurrying over axed their conversation. For now. He stepped aside as Kierra filled the police in about her history with Jonathan.

*J*onathan had certainly changed physically since Kierra had last seen him. The dark circles under his eyes marked loss of sleep; his slimmer waist either indicated less of an appetite or more exercise. For all she knew, he might have been ill. And his behavior clearly indicated a changed person, a true stranger to the one she'd once fallen in love with. It didn't matter. He wanted her back in his life. She wanted him out, permanently.

By the time the officers pulled out of the driveway her family and Ryan surrounded her. They were there for her. Praise God for His strengthening of family ties...and for Ryan. She swallowed hard. For his friendship, never mind what she hoped in addition.

Like a mama bird putting a protective wing around her little one, Anna pulled Kierra into her side. "What's going on? Don't sugarcoat it."

"Jonathan had said a few off things. I was about to phone the cops, but Tessa thankfully beat me to it." Her gaze swept to each of her loving family members, then to Bella, and lingered on Ryan a moment before returning to her mom. "Let's just drop it. Jonathan's gone. It's over."

"He has two legs, a car...can get here any time he wants to." Tessa pulled her hair off her neck. "Goodness, Kierra, if he can drop by after all this time, then open your eyes that he has the gall to harass you more."

Her sister's words stabbed Kierra's spine with chills. She pulled loose from her mom. Funny how she'd longed for Anna to hold her and comfort her, as well as for Tessa's sisterly comfort, yet she was sidestepping away. She needed time alone to process what had just happened with Jonathan, to think of explanations and possibilities.

She gulped.

Just like Ryan had needed privacy when he overheard his

daughter speaking the troubling news of her moving to Colorado with her mother. Kierra was no different.

Her mom narrowed the distance between them. "What did you tell the officers?"

Kierra breathed deeply. Nope. The attempt to relax failed. She pressed down on her lip as fear niggled away her resolve that things would be fine. Jonathan might come back.

Ryan stood a few feet away. His squinty eyes and lowered brows signaled concern, yet she couldn't help but recognize a look of compassion. He did care about her.

She glanced at Tessa whose worry lines furrowing her forehead pulled her back into focus. "I told Jonathan clearly that things are over between us, and to stay away. The police have the necessary information to keep an eye out for him as well. It will be fine." Like a calming ripple over a pond, she paused to let her last few words wash over her.

"How do you know? Remember the trouble I had with Dan? How I had to get a restraining order against him despite the turmoil because he's Zoe's father?"

"That was different. You were married to Dan."

"But Jonathan just proved he's a certified creep."

Kierra placed her hands on her sister. "I love you, Tessa. I'm sorry I haven't said that enough over the years." She sniffled. "Listen, the police told me about my right to issue what's known as a Defiant Trespass Letter, as well as to obtain a Protection from Abuse and Stalking if need be."

Tessa held her at arm's-length. "Doesn't showing his ugly face on your property count as *need be*?"

Kierra glanced at her mom inches away. In her peripheral vision she also saw Zoe and Bella. Her heart sagged more. The girls were way too young to be hearing these details. Somehow, she'd have to take them aside and talk to them about what they were witnessing before they grew wary from fright.

She looked at Tessa. "I don't like the idea that Jonathan

dropped by, but the police stated that first he'd have to complete two separate acts of abuse or stalking before I legally can go after him. Presently, it's a case of him showing up, albeit uninvited, and shooting off his mouth."

"In my book, that's more than enough reason to protect yourself now before it's too late." Tessa reached for her shoulder. "I love you, sis. Do you promise to take care of yourself?"

"Yes. And I promise to take this whole matter seriously." Ryan's focus on her again caught her attention. "Pardon me," she whispered into Tessa's ear. "I'm in need of a private conversation with a good guy. Would you take Mom and the girls inside? There's homemade chocolate pudding pie in the fridge...and several DVDs of chick flicks to watch."

"Sure thing."

Kierra waited until her family and Bella retreated inside. Ironically, she was thankful that her only inn guest was Ryan, and that they had the place to themselves.

She took a few steps toward this special man, reached out for his hand, and breathed a sigh of relief when he grasped her fingers.

23

*T*hey might have kept silent as they walked toward the painted white gazebo on the far side of the lawn, but Kierra felt certain Ryan heard her heart skipping beats.

As they entered the small pavilion with its view of Kindred Lake a blue jay latched onto the attached birdfeeder for a peck of food. A beautiful bird; its bright coat marked it as male. They both sat on the wrap around bench, with no distance between them. Kierra looked at Ryan seated to her right. Would she ever think of him as *her* man...or more?

"I'm glad we're together," she said. "We need to talk."

He grinned. "When a man hears that a woman needs to talk you know he interprets that as trouble, right?"

She could tell he was playing with her, but she held onto the solemn moment.

"Don't worry, you're not in trouble."

He wiped his brow in exaggeration. "That's a relief, especially since I deserve to be for walking away from you back at the park earlier."

"There's a lot happening." She didn't like her own generalization and rushed before he could say more. "What a day. First we're enjoying major fun biking and picnicking and feeling warm and fuzzy...like a real family. Well, at least I felt that way."

"I hear you."

She paused to adore his face. He amazed her. For someone with a myriad of concerns, he remained strong. She admired his strength, his way of exuding calm while pulled apart in various directions. He had this sparkle about him, in his eyes, in his whole being, which she'd never encountered in others.

"Mind if I side-step for a second?"

He shook his head.

"How do you do stay calm among problems?"

"Me?" He lifted a brow. "I had a meltdown after the Baltimore fires and left the news biz. I walked off on you during our outing this afternoon. Definitely not admirable behavior."

"You had good reasons. If I were in your shoes and witnessed what you did in those fires, I would have left my job, or at least taken a serious extended leave of absence." She looked at the blue jay that again busied himself at the feeder. "And I'm sorry I went off on you earlier. Call me selfish, but I admit I was stuck on me...wanting you around."

"I'm glad you do."

"I want more." She closed her eyes then opened them. "There. I said it."

He pulled her tight against him. "I feel the same way about you."

Before they continued on the topic of pursuing a relationship, a question rushed out. "How did you manage to take that walk after you heard Bella with her bombshell news about moving out west, and then return pretty much levelheaded and concerned about me?"

He leaned back and stretched his long legs out. "Want the simple but complex answer?"

"Absolutely."

"God and I talked for a while. Well, more like He talked and I listened. He wants me to accept His love and stop questioning it. And that means I must trust Him, that He makes no mistakes."

"That's a lot to be grateful for, considering I'm learning day by day that I can't handle life on my own."

"I hear you," he said. "His love for me is mind-boggling. I'm an earthly mess of a person that acts dishonorably and constantly put His love for me to shame."

"Yet God loves you no matter what you do—loves each one of us. His only condition—to use a human term—is to love Him back."

"That spells awesome to me."

She rested her head on his shoulder. "Do you believe today's events were meant to occur?"

"I haven't a clue why things happen, but I'm bumping up my trust that God will work it out in good ways my limited human mind can't imagine."

"Like how leaning on your shoulder is comforting? Like us close and cozy after hours of tension between us?"

"Like me kissing you?" He swept his lips over hers.

With his delicious kiss, images of Jonathan, demanding and grousing, were carried off on dandelion fluff to distant shores. Reflections about Kindred Lake Inn's long-term success, and her family's future, also banished. What mattered this second was the flame building between them, one with the potential of more.

"Sweet," Ryan said in a thick breath. "That's what you are."

She moaned. "I was thinking the same about you."

A harsh jaay-jaay trill cut through the air. Kierra turned in time to see the bird fly off to a nearby tree.

"Stupid bird." He chuckled and leaned back on the bench. "Since this romantic moment is ruined, can we talk more about my situation with Bella? I'd love to hear your thoughts."

She straightened and smoothed out her blouse. "What I see is a dad who loves his once estranged daughter. You two have grown closer, even if both of you don't realize it yet. Your relationship may be healing, yet is still fragile. Am I way off base?"

"You're spot on."

"Whew. Realize I'm proceeding with caution because I don't have children of my own and don't want—"

He squeezed her hand. "No need for a warning label. You're a kindhearted human being. That's what counts."

"My opinion is that since your ex hasn't phoned to share definite plans you should continue to spend quality time with Bella. You might want to be honest and tell her that you've overheard her and Zoe speaking. Share your thoughts. Invite her to share her feelings. This way you can establish firmer ground with each other and by doing so, become prepared if and when her mom does go through with this move to Colorado. By doing so, you and Bella aren't thrown together in a chaotic tumble of raw emotions."

"Good idea. May I include you in our activities?"

She smiled. "Of course, as long as you spend alone time together with each other."

He sprang to his feet and crossed to the gazebo's opening where he peered at the lake. In a flash, she was beside him.

"What are you thinking?" She slipped an arm around his waist. And waited.

"Reporting the news, both the beautiful and the ugly, has taught me a lot about life, like expecting the unexpected. I thought I mastered that lesson." He faced her. "When I heard Bella tell Zoe about moving away I nearly stopped breathing. And though you might have seen me walk away to think, believe me, it was an effort and a half to put one foot in front of the other and to move forward."

"You didn't freeze, though."

"I came close, which I don't want to ever experience again. I love my daughter, and don't want to ever, ever let her down." He paused. "A husband, father, and friend shouldn't be a disappointment to those he loves."

"Hey, Aunt Kierra. Hey, Ryan."

They both turned to see Zoe trotting toward them. Not ready for a teen interrogation, Kierra inched a respectable distance from Ryan.

Zoe stepped into the gazebo. "Grandma says dinner's ready."

"Already?" Kierra glanced at her watch. She leaned toward Ryan's ear to whisper. "Time flies when you're falling for a handsome man."

Zoe cleared her throat on the loud side. "Grandma will be ticked if you two are late. I'll meet you back at the inn." A flush spread across her face and she took off.

Ryan tugged her closer. "Must be all the biking, walking...and falling for each other that we did today, but I'm starved. Ready?"

"Yep." She was indeed ready to go back to the historic house that had become her home and business. Ready to get to know him and his daughter better. She loved how he brought God into the picture, how they needed to trust Him. With that in mind, casting her fears and concerns aside, she walked by his side, hand in hand, to the dinner awaiting them. Things had a way of working out for the best.

24

*B*efore retreating for the evening to her private apartment over the carriage house, Kierra made her routine check through the inn. On the way downstairs the bright kitchen light halted her steps. Tessa and Zoe's voices, though soft, sailed into the hallway. She didn't want to eavesdrop; yet she felt awkward barging in on a mother-daughter moment.

"I can't sleep," Zoe said. "But, Mom, you look like you haven't tried."

"You're right. I've never been good at concealing my feelings from you."

"From anyone."

"Isn't that the truth?" Chair legs scraped the oak floor and a wooden thump filled the otherwise quiet of the night. "Come sit beside me, Zoe."

"Are you worrying about what happened earlier?" Zoe asked. "It was a pretty cool day, until the cops came."

"Don't fret about your old mom."

"You're not old."

"You're the sweetest, hon."

"Can I do your nails? I want to do something nice for you. You know, maybe end a weird day on a jazzier note."

"It's after midnight," Tessa said in a high-pitched squawk. "If I were a good mom I'd escort you to your bed right now."

"You are a great mom and I can prove that."

"How?"

"Because." Zoe's tone was heaver, more serious. "You're letting me stay with you right now. You know, I'm glad we moved here. We were, like, a whole different mother and daughter. Like at war with each other. All. The. Time."

A sniffle. "And now?"

"We're more like family."

A half chuckle, half groan came. Tessa's trademark sound when emotions swirled her dizzy. "That's the loveliest thing I've heard in a long time."

"Then why are you crying? Should I get Grandma?"

"No, no. Let her sleep." Another sniffle then snort. "When you're a grown woman you'll master sobbing through beautiful times."

"That's silly."

A loud smooch smacked the air.

"Hey, what's that for, Mom?"

"For making me happy. If you want to do my nails, go for it."

"Yay. Since we're awake, we might as well have fun. Stay here. I'll be right back."

Kierra slipped into the dark laundry room. Seconds later the flooring squeaked from her niece's jog down the hallway.

Aware that her entrance into the kitchen might ruin Tessa's time with Zoe, Kierra's own inner knots shouted that she needed a sister-to-sister time. She rushed to the kitchen.

"Me and Zoe," Tessa mumbled to herself. "I never thought that was possible until moving here."

"Knock, knock," Kierra said at the doorway. "Can I come in?"

Tessa jumped and placed her hand on her gray sweatshirt over her heart. "Of course. This is your place."

"I don't want to intrude." Kierra hurried in and grabbed the chair beside her sister.

Tessa smirked. "Says she who hesitated not a second longer."

Kierra eyed the vacant seat on the opposite side of the table. "Was someone else here?"

Her sis bobbed her head. "Zoe. She'll return in a flash. She wants to polish my nails. Can you imagine?"

"Aw, that's sweet." Kierra fidgeted with the yellow placemat before her. "I should gather drinks and a snack. I have pretzels. They're store-bought, not home-baked."

"You don't have to play the forever hostess."

"I like fussing over you."

Tessa narrowed her eyes.

"Don't look at me that way. I'm thinking how..." She glanced away, the stovetop a sudden diversion.

Tessa touched her shoulder. "What?"

"How lonely I'll be without the three of you with me."

"Turn around and look at your old sis."

"First old mom, now old sis. What is it about age and you?" Kierra shrieked. "Oops."

"Just as I thought...and hoped. You were outside of the kitchen listening in."

"Guilty." Kierra lowered her head then snapped it upright. "Did you say hoped?"

"Yeah, you heard right. In the back of my mind as Zoe and I talked I kept wishing you were here. I mean, my time with her defined precious in a way I'd never known, but I thought how cool it would be to have a sister-mother-daughter-auntie time."

"Way overdue."

"Very much so."

"What's overdue?" Zoe asked as she zoomed over and

plopped three bottles of nail polish onto the table. "Hi, Aunt Kierra."

Kierra smiled at her niece, also wearing gray sweats like her mom. "How nice it is that we can spend time together."

The outside door slid open then shut. "Ah, the miles of unlimited country roads and scenic vistas to explore. That's one big and bodacious advantage of moving to Kindred Lake."

"Mom," Kierra and Tessa said in unison.

"You couldn't sleep either, Grandma?" Zoe slid the chair beside her out from the table. "Sit next to me."

Anna toed her shoes off, but kept on her green fleece vest she wore over a soft blue peasant-styled blouse. She hurried over. "It was muddy besides the lake."

"Oh, Mom," Kierra said. "Although Kindred Lake is one of the few remaining American sleepy towns with the perk of a low crime rate, you shouldn't go walking by the lake alone at this time of night."

"I'm perfectly fine. I can hold my own." Anna winked at Zoe. "Grandma can slay dragons, clobber giants over the head with her gourmet frying pan, and bore the life out of questionable strangers by reciting old blog posts about the merits of using olive oil."

Kierra shook her head. "Mom, seriously?"

"Darling, I am serious. Besides, I ran into your tall and dark haired gorgeous friend."

"Ryan," Zoe said as if his name was an exclamation point. "He's also awake? Guess no one can sleep."

Tessa leaned back. "What a day we had."

"Where is he?" Kierra asked.

Tessa ribbed her in the side. "Curious, are we?"

"Look at my two daughters getting along." Anna beamed. "Your inn guest was out walking by the lake when we met. He then received a text from his upset daughter. He asked Bella that if her mom allowed, if she'd like for him to get her and bring her here to hang out."

Kierra couldn't hold back a second longer. "And?"

"He's on his way over to get Bella."

"Quick," Zoe said. "Let's get this girls' slumber party rockin'." She scooped up the bottles full of polish. "I have black, white, and purple. Who's first?"

"Me...me," Tessa squealed. "I've waited a life and a half for my little girl to offer to glam me up and I'm not sidestepping out of line for either my mom or sis to grab my spot."

Anna changed seats with Tessa and gave Kierra a hearty embrace. "Hear this loud and clear, my darling daughters and granddaughter: We need to do this more often. Let's not wait for a rough day to pull us together. Agree?"

Everyone nodded.

"Mom, stop squirming or I'll ruin your nails." Zoe dipped the brush into the black polish. "Since you didn't tell me what you want, I'll paint each nail half black and half white."

"That's awesome, hon."

Anna hummed a few bars of a song Kierra hadn't heard in years, but couldn't place.

"I'm in the mood for love," Tessa sang, as if reading Kierra's thoughts. She wrinkled her forehead and looked at Zoe. "I can't recall the rest of the words. Do you know them, babe?"

"Babe?" Zoe giggled. "Simply because we don't have to spend our allowance on love," she sang out to the tune of the old song.

"Amen," Tessa said. "That's so true."

"Mom, I'm happy doing this for you."

Tessa batted her lashes. "You're going to make me cry again."

"Why's that?"

"You're making me remember happy times that I haven't thought about in years. Like learning that I was pregnant with you." With her free hand Tessa rubbed her belly. "Like feeling you move for the first time within me."

Zoe sat back. "Am I supposed to say aw or yuck? I'm confused."

"Considering your age, either one." Tessa tugged Zoe into her arms and kissed her forehead. "You always make me happy, and that's what counts. I just haven't told you enough."

Zoe touched the spot where her mom kissed as if it were the first time. "Your nails..." She pulled back. "Wait. I *always* make you happy?"

"You do, and that doesn't matter if I'm upset with you or you're upset with me. In other words, sweetheart, my love isn't conditional based upon your actions. I'm sorry I've never spelled it out in these simple terms."

Zoe shrugged. "I guess that's another woman thing I'll understand eventually when I'm older...or a mom myself."

"Don't rush into womanhood, hon. It will happen fast enough."

"Well, Mom," Zoe said with a slight whine. "Looks like your nails held up, after all. Do you want me to apply hearts, stars, or daisies?"

Tessa peered across the table at Kierra and their mom. "What do you think?"

"Your choice," Kierra said.

"Hearts." Tessa placed both hands on the placemat. "I'm ready."

Anna leaned toward Kierra. "Are these mats good ones?"

"Not a problem, Mom. I can replace them, if need be. What I can't replace is this evening with all of you."

"Mother!" Zoe said in a mock scolding tone. "You must stop biting your nails. What will others think?"

Tessa grabbed Zoe's right hand. "Fine. I'll munch on yours."

Zoe laughed hard as Tessa pretended to crunch her hands.

With care and precision, Zoe applied the stick-on design to her mom's nails. She finished each nail with purple squiggly lines on alternate fingers for accent.

"What do you think, Mom? Are they funky enough?"

Tessa studied her nails. "Superb job. I love them. Thank you." She offered her hands for Kierra and Anna's inspection, and smiled at their admiration.

"Who's next," Zoe asked, stifling a yawn.

The outside door opened.

"Are we interrupting?" Ryan said.

"Not at all," Kierra said. "You're a guest, so come on in." She stepped toward the fridge. "It's hours away from breakfast time, but I can easily fix us eggs if anyone's hungry."

"Have you any ham?"

Kierra hesitated, not expecting that question. Tired, she'd been thinking easy, not fancy.

A grin crossed Ryan's lips. "I can make a pretty good ham strata, if you'd like."

Oh, she liked, all right, but she wasn't thinking necessarily only about food. She pulled out a mixing bowl and the ingredients. Any man who would cook for her was a winner. No, that wasn't right. Not any, but this particular one. "Go for it."

"Ryan?" Anna called from the table. "I thought you said you were getting Bella."

"I did..." He glanced about the kitchen. His face turned ashen. "Must find my daughter. Pardon me." He darted outdoors before anyone could respond.

25

𝓡yan strode toward the lake in hope of finding his daughter. He remembered as a kid he'd always chose a private place to hash matters out; Kindred Lake was pretty private. As he made his way toward the water he took in the sight of the gazebo. Under the full moon the white painted structure glowed.

Hours ago, when alone with Kierra, he'd let himself get carried away during one of their kisses and dared to let his imagination rip. He imagined that under the gazebo's roof he'd wrap her in his arms and promise to protect her from the darkness of evening. A strong, independent woman, she didn't need a proverbial knight in shining armor to guard over her, but he liked the idea of keeping her safe from harm's way. They would nestle tighter in an embrace. They'd go on to share dreams, let go of their pasts, and explore new possibilities. After laughter and whispers of love talk, she'd take his hand and lead him into a waltz played by the musicians only their ears could hear.

What was happening to him? Until the horrific Baltimore fires he'd always been a control freak, not in structuring and commanding others but rather, a true self-disciplinarian. With the death of the little innocent girl, he'd lost it. He walked off the job, stopped exercising and biking, stopped finding joy in life. He'd come close to surrendering his faith in God, but couldn't quite let go. In hindsight, he could see how God wouldn't let go of him. And praise Him for His grip on him. Slowly, he'd managed to push himself to get out of his four walls and into physical shape again. Slowly, his mind freed. He realized both he and his daughter weren't getting younger and it was time to mend the emotional distance already separating them. Then, he'd met Kierra.

He'd lost control with her as well, but unlike the fires and its aftermath, this swirly, giddy and luscious sensation was a beyond positive high. He was falling...

Hold on a sec. Falling?

As in *falling in love*?

The closest he'd come to letting go and loving a woman was Lisa. They'd married and he thought their love would last forever. This thing that encompassed each cell in his body, that fueled him with an immeasurable energy, that buzzed him with joy, this he'd never experienced with his wife. A jewel did come out of their union...

His daughter.

He stopped his march toward the lake and beside the gazebo rested his eyes closed.

Bella. She was the only one who mattered.

"Hey, Dad."

"Bella?" She sat on the wrap around bench seat, arms hugging her knees. The way her long hair flowed over her shoulders probably added a little warmth from the chilly air, but she'd neglected to wear a jacket. He took off his and wrapped it around her. "You all right?"

"Now that you're here, yeah."

"Good." He waited for her to continue, but she remained silent. "Busy thinking?"

She shrugged. "Kind of. I have stuff to share with you, but you won't like it."

"Don't worry about what I like or not. Let's hear whatever you want to talk about."

She swung her feet to the wooden floor. He sat beside her.

"I'm glad you're in town for a visit."

"It's long overdue."

"I hate what made you come, though."

He put an arm around her and discovered she was trembling a little. He pulled her tighter to his side. "That I let those fires get under my skin...that I gave up on a good career?"

She shook her head, her hair flying over his shirt. "No, because in my eyes it's way different. You see yourself as a loser, Dad, but that's not how I see you."

He swallowed hard, and waited for her to continue.

She ran her tongue over her lips. "Anyone that experienced what you did with those fires and then witnessed the death of that child would have flipped. But not you."

"That's sweet of you to say, but most adults don't see it that way. I stepped away from a good job. Despite standing on sturdier feet these days, I'm still seen by those in the news business as someone unable to handle difficulties. In their eyes I'm a wash-up, a has-been."

"Stop it." She jumped to her feet and faced him with crossed arms. "You'll have to decide whether those fancy connections and what they say and think count more than what I say and think." She stared hard at him. "Tell me the truth why you're in Kindred Lake when you can be wherever you want?"

"I'm here to see you."

"Why?"

"Because I love you, Bella. You're my daughter."

She moved to the gazebo's entrance and stared off into the night's darkness. "I'm glad you love me. And I love you. But you're here because of Mom, because you two are divorced, and because she won't take me to visit you, you have to come north to visit me." She faced him. "What I hate is that the two of you are divorced. I hate that you were once happy, but then I came along and your marriage went downhill."

He crossed over to stand beside her. "Sweetheart, you weren't the cause of your mom and I ending our marriage."

She sagged. He pulled her into a hug.

"No, that's not what I mean, either." She let out a twisted sigh. "I know what you caught Mom doing, you know, with the other guy. It was wrong. And the funny thing is, he's totally out of the picture, has been for years. But the thing is you have to visit with me. And it's because of me that Mom has to make these arrangements to share me, like I'm some sort of thing, not a person."

"You're no thing, sweetheart. You're my treasured prize in life."

She pulled back. "Totally awesome."

Teenagers and their sarcasm. He resisted reacting. "What's troubling you?"

"Because Mom and Alex are moving to Colorado after they get hitched in July. Mom thinks it's best if I go with her, and attend a new school. And be with Alex's supposedly cool family. Like that's happening. Not."

This wasn't the best timing to bring up the fact that he'd overheard her mention this to Zoe. "I've known your mom and Alex had become engaged, but didn't know about them marrying in a few months. Good for them. We both have to accept she has full-time custody. I'm restricted to visitation, holiday and vacation times." To think this was based upon his long ago decision to advance his career, one that no longer existed. He inwardly sighed. This conversation wasn't getting easier. He willed himself to remain levelheaded. "If she believes it's in your best interest then we should give it a bit of consideration, at least hear her out. We can agree upon a solution to make everyone happy."

"But I like this town. I finally made a friend...Zoe." Bella turned her back on him. "And with Kierra...it's like..."

"What, honey?"

"Zoe and I saw you two kissing. I kind of acted weird, like I wasn't cool about it, but I really was. Know why?"

He and Kierra shouldn't have let their passion get carried away in public, but restraint wasn't easy around her. But he needed to confront his daughter. He'd bank on the truth as the only option.

"Kierra is a beautiful woman, both personality and looks wise."

"Yeah, and that's the thing, Dad. This is the first time I'm seeing you happy with someone totally awesome. It was the first time that I let myself dream what it would be like if you two married and I lived with you and had her as a stepmom, and the three of us lived under one roof, full-time, together." She sighed again. "I'm thinking that because of me, once again, things will be messy for you. I bet I'm already getting in the way."

He squeezed her shoulder. "Bella, you're not getting between me and anyone. Listen carefully—you're the only one that counts in my life. You're my number one. I won't be happy unless you're happy."

*S*tep by step, Kierra backed away from the tall bushes alongside the gazebo where Ryan and Bella stood. The shrubbery might have kept her hidden from father and daughter, but failed to block their voices from reaching her ears.

As if anesthetized, her mind went numb. It was safer this way, easier to handle than a stampede of thoughts, and raw emotions.

Time slipped by. She didn't recall walking into her kitchen then finding her way to the table. She slumped onto a chair and squeezed her eyes shut.

A hand pressed upon her shoulder.

"Tessa and Zoe have gone back to their rooms, hon," Anna

said. "It's just us. I'll leave if you want your privacy, though not before you tell me you're okay."

Kierra dragged her hands down her face then glanced at her mother. "I'm fine, as well as Ryan and Bella."

Her mom remained silent.

"You're not believing me?"

"No," Anna said, tenderly. "You're pretty upset for me to believe all is well."

Kierra leaned back. "I'm probably upset because I'm tired." She glanced at the wall clock. "Yikes. Four a.m. I've been up the whole night. No surprise I'm anxious."

"Upsetting events can weigh one down."

"That's a statement and a half." Kierra fixed her sight on the teakettle on the stovetop. "You're right. This was a crazy day."

"Honey, seeing Jonathan, especially his antagonistic behavior toward you, rates high in the troubles department."

"His whole appearance and behavior definitely came out of nowhere."

"Yes, it did. Yet, I'm sensing there's more perplexing you."

"I don't know...I don't understand what's happening."

Anna rubbed Kierra's back in the slow circular strokes she remembered from childhood.

"Mom, I'm glad you're back in my life."

"I was never away," Anna murmured. "A bit pre-occupied with my own interests, I admit. Let's go onward into life, together."

Kierra sniffled. "I'd like that, Mom."

A beat of silence ticked by; the refrigerator's motor kicked in adding a buzz throughout the kitchen.

"What happened out there?" Anna asked.

"It's nothing...I'm confused."

"You're covering up, and I don't think it's for someone else but rather it's for you."

She eyed her mom. "I'm not following."

"My mom-intuition tells me you're denying a batch of pretty strong feelings...and I'm thinking it's over someone."

"Well, I was concerned over Ryan finding Bella. Those two have a fragile relationship and I'm nervous for them."

Anna fanned her fingertips across Kierra's cheek. "And?"

Kierra sat straighter, the truth obvious and powerful. "I'm in love with Ryan."

"He's a good soul."

"But I don't know him."

"You know enough to love what you see. Did you know that Gram married Grandpa two months after they met?" Anna grinned. "And no, it's not because I was on the way. Gram knew. She loved your grandfather, and he loved her. And me? Your dad and I dated for a year and a half before we married and look what happened."

"Are you saying the moral of this story is that you can't tell what will happen in life?"

"What I'm trying to say is that love is worth taking a chance. Gram and Grandpa loved each other. And yes, I loved your dad. Gram took a chance after barely knowing him. I took a chance on Dad after thinking I knew him inside and out over a year's time."

Kierra stared at her mom's bare ring finger, the one she couldn't remember ever adorned by a wedding band. "Dad divorced you when I was five. You guys fought a lot, and you were sad all the time, and you remained unhappy after the divorce."

"Yes, you're right." Anna breathed out a long breath. "You were too young to remember, but our first few years were golden times. Happy times. I loved your dad, and basked in his love for me."

"But, Mom, that love didn't last."

"Certainly not long enough. We began with enough powerful love to take a chance on each other, and that's what counted."

"Any regrets?"

"Not one. Looking back, I can see ways we might have worked

it out, but the past can't be changed." Anna reached for Kierra's hands. "It wasn't until I came to Kindred Lake that I started to relax by thanking God for my blessings. I was a good wife. I was blessed with two beautiful daughters."

"Oh...Mom..."

"I'm just sorry that it's taken me years to show my gratitude to you and your sister."

"What counts is your love. And I love you, Mom."

"You're a good, beautiful daughter. And now you're getting my meaning."

"About love?" Ryan's smiling eyes flashed before her. His rich tenor voice riding on lush musical notes reached her ears. His lips upon hers filled her with warmth that begged for more. She looked at her mom. "Bella's mom and boyfriend are getting married and moving to Colorado. They think it's best if they take her with them. The poor girl is upset." She paused, the thick words weighing down her tongue. "The last thing I want to do is to come across as a self-centered person who steps between a father and his daughter. With Ryan not tied down to a job, I don't know whether he's considering relocating out west or returning to Maryland, but he's certainly not making room in his life for me."

"How do you know?"

"Out by the gazebo, where I found the two of them, I heard Ryan tell Bella that she's the only one that matters in his life."

"Then talk with him. Love's worth the pursuit."

"That makes a nice coffee mug saying, but in real life it's iffy, at least in this situation."

"Don't tell me you're giving up?"

On her feet, Kierra looked about the room where already fond memories were attached to the stove where Ryan prepared food, the table where he sat and shared conversation, the window he glanced out to view the lake. "Thanks, Mom. You've helped me to realize that I can't give up on what actually hasn't developed.

Ryan came to town to heal his relationship with his daughter. On the same day, you and Tessa moved in with me and we began to mend the brokenness between us. That's everything wonderful, a true blessing." She leaned over to kiss her mom then stood.

"Hold on, dear. Guys like Ryan are hard to find. Why not ask him yourself about what he'd told his daughter? A man can love his child as well as a woman." She winked. "Especially one who might become his wife."

"His wife? Isn't that pushing him away from his daughter?"

"If love is big and strong enough, there's plenty for others."

"That's another great coffee mug maxim." She yawned. "I'm turning in for a little shuteye. I hope you get some sleep."

Anna peered into Kierra's eyes. "In a little while. I have some things to think about."

26

No way would Ryan fall asleep, not after dropping an upset Bella off at her mom's. Instead, he slipped out of his shoes at the inn's entrance and carried them as he walked gingerly to the library. He pushed open the door to the handsome room lined with three walls of chest-high glassed-front oak bookcases. The forth wall hosted two red and gold striped wingback chairs that appeared stiff and unwelcoming for his exhausted and drained state of mind. He chose the plump sofa in the center of the room with its inviting big throw pillows and sank onto the left cushion. With an arm tossed over the arm, he stretched his legs before him and set his head on the sofa's back.

He needed to have a long overdue chat with his ex, but how? The one priority that Lisa had made clear through the years was for him to respect her privacy. Upon their divorce, she'd kept a tight-lip on her lifestyle, work, and interests. His reporter's connections discreetly verified that she had at least done everything legit and safe. He didn't care for the overnight boyfriends through the years, but his sources confirmed that outwardly his daughter hadn't suffered. He'd give Lisa this: she would battle legions to ensure no harm came to Bella. And now Lisa was engaged and soon would wed. The couple of times he'd met Alex he came across as pleasant and kind. At least he had a decent job. In fact, he was offered a sizable promotion at the Denver location. Things were finally looking bright for his ex. More than he could have given her, apparently.

Wait a second.

He didn't need to put himself down. He'd done the best he could years back when they married. He had been a good husband. A good father. Lisa chose differently. He needed to remember that...and that things could be different for him in the future.

Like with Kierra?

I'm confused God. Help me.

His gaze strayed across the room to the antique lithograph hung above a bookcase. The print appeared to be in its original gold leaf frame. The subject, a 1800s sailing ship on stormy seawaters, drew his attention. He bounced to his feet for a closer examination.

The old Breton Fisherman's Prayer came to mind. A few years ago on President John F. Kennedy's birthday he'd reported on the old prayer inscribed on a plaque that JFK had kept on his desk in the Oval Office. Weary and in need of the support that only God could give, Ryan bowed his head. Similar to these ancient fishermen on stormy seas, he prayed.

Father, this world is huge and chaotic. I can't handle this myself. Surround those I love, as well as myself, with your protection. Give us the wisdom and the strength to do what only You know is best.

Whenever he prayed he also rested afterwards in the anticipation of God replacing his whirlwind thoughts with His breath of love and peace. This wasn't a time for exception. He pressed his head on top of the bookcase and shut his eyes.

A door creaked open. Footfall followed. The sounds were far away, of no concern of his. Rather, he heard the soft tread of his four-year-old daughter attempting to sneak up on him as he read the newspaper.

"*G*otcha," Bella said, her voice more giggles than syllables.

Ryan gaped his mouth open.

"Did I scare you, Daddy?"

He let out a small groan and thumped his heart. "You most certainly did, my little princess. Do you know what daddies do to their little girls who frighten them?"

Bella eyes widened. She shook her head.

He pulled her over the back of the couch and tickled her. The laughter flowing from her soul shoved away the day's current events exploding around the globe, his to-do list on his day off from work, and his wife's latest complaint slash accusation. He and Bella were alone in the house and all was right in their world.

"Mama had to go shopping. How about if I fix you a snack then we can play a game?"

"What kind of snack? What game?"

He chuckled. "Lots of good questions, sweetheart. Which one do you want to know about first?"

His serious thinker scrunched her forehead. "Snack."

"Ah, I thought so. Carrot sticks or pretzels?"

"Pessels, please."

"Why aren't I surprised?" He slid her off his lap, stood, and grasped her hand. "Do you want to hop or skip our way to the kitchen?"

"Hop." Her expressive face showed a thought clearly giving her pause. "Daddy, you're fun. How come Mama isn't?"

His heart clenched. "She is, just in her own way. Mama loves you so much."

His daughter smiled softly and reached for his hand. "I'm hungry."

"Let's go, partner."

The memory receded. Ryan stood in the present, in the Kindred Lake Inn, the inn owned by a woman he couldn't chase from his thoughts...nor wanted to.

Yet, he heard a different voice speaking.

My son, hold onto your love of others and you won't go wrong.

A touch came to his shoulder.

He cracked open one eye. Anna?

Dressed in the same blue blouse and slacks he'd last seen her in, she appeared composed and calm. Had she slept at all?

"Hi, Ryan. Is there anything I can get you?"

"That's kind of you. I'm fine, though."

"I see." She stepped back. "I'll leave you to yourself. Sorry for the intrusion." She turned and headed to the door.

"Wait." He lifted his chin toward the sofa. "Stay, if you'd like."

"Sure." She waited until he made the first move forward.

A smart woman. He could see Anna's positive influence over both of her daughters, especially Kierra. Eager for the older woman's companionship, he sank onto the sofa.

She sat on the other cushion and waited for him to start the conversation.

"Anna, do you believe in coincidences?"

She propped an elbow onto the sofa's back. "Like me finding you here?"

He tilted his head. "Yeah, let's start with that one."

"There's always two ways of looking at things. I tried to instill that in my daughters when they were young. I wanted them to open their minds to not only their way of thinking but to consider how others may perceive the same situation."

"Wise."

"Often, they didn't think that way." She smirked. "Ah, what do parents know, right?"

"I definitely hear you."

"To answer your question, I see it two different ways. First, is on the physical level. You're awake. I'm awake. Neither one of us are holed up in our separate bedrooms and despite this inn being spacious, we happened across each other." She smiled softly. "Well, at least I found you."

"And the second level?"

"It was meant to happen. Whether one believes in coincidences or a cosmic matter directing people and places and timing."

"I believe God is active in our lives." He believed strongly in God and felt comfortable with Anna in sharing his faith. "I believe His hands are always on my back leading me."

"I agree. So back to your question, no, I'm not a fan of chance random coincidences or encounters. Why do you ask?"

"I have a lot on my mind."

"Bella?"

He wanted to reply yes. Of course he always thought about his daughter. But, a different name rolled from his mouth.

"Kierra."

Anna surprised him with silence. Her calm eyes and smooth brow indicated she was neither surprised nor upset by her daughter's mention.

He glanced again at he lithograph of the ship on the sea. "Where to begin?"

"Beginnings are usually a great place, but I'm thinking it's the middle of your story that has you spinning a bit."

He snapped his head around to face her. "You have keen perception, Anna."

"Thanks. If only my daughters realized that years ago, but that's a whole different subject."

He crossed his arms then uncrossed then. He no longer could hold back. Didn't want to. If anyone could help to clarify his standing with Kierra, he'd think it would be her mom.

"I have this thing for your daughter." He winced. "Yikes. I sound like a teenager."

"Falling in love can do that to a person...not saying you love Kierra...but..." She smiled warmly without judgment clouding her eyes.

"Middle of the story, not the beginning, huh?" He thought for a moment then plunged right in. "A while back an awful experience shook me. It made me realize how precious life, namely my daughter, is. I hopped on my bike and came to town to mend things with Bella, never expecting to meet Kierra. Never expecting to..." He needed to articulate his feelings, as if expressing them made them more real. Just when he opened his mouth to speak, Anna interjected.

"Saying things aloud brings an internal emotion into an external reality."

He lifted a brow.

She gave a little shake of her head. "No shrink, just a mom."

"You're amazing," he murmured. "I was just thinking that. No offense to your kitchen skills, but do consider hosting a parenting blog rather than a food one. You're guaranteed to have a huge following."

"Well, thank you. There's a thought. No offense taken."

"I've fallen in love with Kierra." He'd expected the confession to unsettle him, but the opposite occurred: it calmed his soul. "We might not have known each other for long, but it takes a special woman for me to admire and love."

"Is this a problem?"

"I don't want to hurt your daughter."

Anna's smile faded. "How can your love hurt her?"

He rubbed the side of his head. "It could be a case of the right thing at the wrong time. Bella's upset because she has to move to

Colorado when her mom marries in July. My daughter needs my support, which I need—and want to—rev up more because I owe it to her as her dad. And then there's me."

"You?"

"I'm presently without a job. As you may know, I left behind an excellent career to give myself a mental holiday of sorts."

"Recovery is a good thing."

"But every wife deserves a husband who isn't a slacker."

She blinked. "Have you proposed to Kierra?"

"No. But I don't believe in a casual relationship without long-term commitment." He half laughed, half groaned. "Probably why the few dates I've had since my divorce never went far."

"That might be a good thing."

He leaned forward. "And your advice?"

She fingered the upholstery on the sofa's back. "If you pay attention to your priorities, and your heart, you won't go wrong."

A crash came from the hallway. Ryan and Anna sprang to their feet.

"No," Kierra shouted, the word stretched far longer than the two letters in the word and sailed past the library door that Anna had left open.

Ryan stepped into the hallway in time to see Kierra fling a canister against the wall. Pens flew out and puddled alongside the guest book already sprawled on the floor, its pages ruffled.

27

"*L*isten carefully because I'm about to hang up. Do not phone again." Kierra might have had a lecture or two rolled up her sleeve, but dared not waste one more breath on the wacko. She clicked off the phone, thankful her mom and Ryan stood beside her.

"Sorry for the drama," she said as she glanced at the mess on the floor she'd created. "Guess I vented a wee on the loud side."

"I'd do the same, or worse." Anna touched her arm softly. "You don't sound at ease, though."

"How would you react if you'd just received a prank call on zilch hours of sleep?" Shame lifted from her chest and flamed her face. "Sorry, Mom. I shouldn't have snapped." In need of physical support she leaned against the hallway desk.

Ryan reached for her shoulder. "Let me help."

Only a little while ago she'd chatted with her mom and concluded she wouldn't swoon over Ryan's looks, or yearn for his touch. But now? If he moved an inch closer the cuff of his long sleeve would brush her cheek... would an electric charge jump from his fingers to her if he were to fan them across her face?

She glanced about. Her mom had slipped away.

"She wanted to give us our privacy," Ryan said.

Privacy? Why? They had nothing to talk about. "Silly Mom." She eyed the phone. "It was just an annoying kid playing a game. I tend to overreact when sleep-deprived. Not my prettiest moment."

"You're shaking." He pulled her against his chest.

She didn't wiggle away. He was steady to her wobbliness, grounded to her pretense that nothing bad had occurred.

"Want to share?"

She shook her head then nodded. His shirt buttons tickled her forehead.

"Was it Jonathan?"

"I'm unsure." Her reply sounded ridiculous to her own ears. She'd been engaged to Jonathan and yet she couldn't quite pin him as the caller. "Whoever it was said weird stuff, things I couldn't imagine Jonathan saying."

"Are we talking about the same person that showed with flowers in hand, refusing to budge when you told him to leave?"

She leaned back. "Point taken."

"I have a daughter who visits because I'm a paying guest." He glanced around the reception area. "You live here as well, and have family staying for an indefinite time period. I need to know if this is a prank that can be ignored or a true threat."

A daughter who visits...Ryan a paying guest...her own family to consider. He was right. She owed him an explanation. But first, she needed to take matters into her own hands and confront the truth, and to trust that God would answer her prayers to protect those she loved.

"You're right again." She slipped her purse off of the nearby coat tree. "I'll be back shortly with those answers." She opened the front door.

"Wait..."

She dashed toward her car, each second too precious to squander.

28

*R*elief flooded Kierra when she glanced at the rearview mirror and didn't see Ryan following her. This defining moment in life may fall under the category of risks, but better late than never. As daring as it was, she needed to do this entirely on her own.

She right-turned into Jonathan's driveway. His Kia sat centered before the garage leaving her with no space to park. The front door to the brick two-story house she came close to calling home opened as she backed out to the street. Two choices pressed heavily on her shoulders. She could step on the gas and skedaddle back to the inn. Or, swallow her trepidation and get out of the car and march forward to speak with Jonathan.

She slipped from the car and gave a little wave to her former fiancé. He waved back with the friendliest of smiles as if anticipating her arrival.

Dressed in a brown bathrobe cinched over a pair of jeans, he leaned against one of the portico's column. "Nice to see you again, lovey."

"Please, Jonathan. My name's fine, but no endearments."

"I can't imagine what this is about. Would you like to come in?

I can brew us a pot of coffee." He glanced at his watch. "If you haven't had breakfast yet, I'll throw together some eggs and cinnamon rolls."

Food and she weren't buddies right then. "No thanks. Let's talk outdoors."

"If that's what you prefer." He stuffed his hands in his pockets. "I'd like to believe this is about you coming to your senses and wanting to make up and to get on with our lives together, but I'm guessing it's not."

She chose to ignore his little dig about her waking up to accommodate his desires. Pick a battle, as the saying went. She also opted to stay put, the distance between them, if only a few feet, a little comforting. "It's over between us. We must accept this and move forward."

"We?" He pursed his lips. "See, that's the thing. A relationship is a two-way street."

"I agree. And I'm out of it, have been since we've called off our wedding."

"And I want back in. You can't simply negate me out of the equation."

He might be lonely, hurt, and if anything, definitely confused. Yet, he was a person with feelings and she needed to be kind and levelheaded. "Jonathan, tell me about how life's been treating you since we broke up."

His shoulders drooped. "Wow, that question came out of nowhere."

"When you think about it, not really. I don't hate you." His sudden smile boosted the tension swirling within her. She pushed to explain. "Yeah, it's quits between us, but I'm wishing you the best. I want you to be happy and hope you want the same for me."

"I'd be happy with you back in my life," he said softly. He watched two robins land on the birdbath on the far side of the lawn. "Seems like everyone and everything has a mate."

An *oh-Jonathan* bubbled from her throat to her mouth but he beat her to words.

"You asked about me in the game of life. Not great, but not horrible. Work's going well—I just made tenure in the math department. I'm healthy. Socially, I've dated a few nice women, but there's no one like you, lovey."

Her heart squeezed. "I'm glad things are good for you. As far as women go, the perfect one for you is out there and I'm sure you'll meet her." When that solid look of his remained fixed on her, she wanted to walk away, but this conversation needed to continue. "I'm not the right one for you. I might want children one day, might want—"

"That's the only regret I have."

She tamped back her resentment. "The vasectomy?"

"My disappointments don't hover over not wanting children, but rather, of upsetting you. We should have talked about this before I made my unilateral decision. That's where I went wrong."

Surprise shot through her. "No, that was only part of it. You've helped me to realize what is important to me."

"Like children?"

She tilted her head. "What's most important to me is honesty and trust." Her words summoned images of Ryan. He'd shared his honest feelings, the good, the messy, and the awful. She trusted him, and believed he trusted her as well.

Her cell vibrated in her pants pocket with an incoming text. She ignored it. "I tried to express myself clearly that day of your procedure, and those following days. Our emotions were heated big time."

His eyes clouded with a faraway look. "They were."

"Jonathan, it's not your fault, nor mine, that our engagement didn't work. It's not like we cheated on each other or were physically abusive or discovered a nasty habit the other had. It ended because it wasn't meant to be. And that's a good thing."

He lifted a brow.

"Yes," she said in reinforcement. "Best we called it off rather than go through years of marriage yelling and crying, don't you think?"

"You don't hate me?"

She'd come close to it when he'd threatened to chase after her and her family during his phone call earlier—if Jonathan had indeed been the caller—but she could see this face-to-face talk hit home with him.

She rushed to him, gave him a fast hug, and then stepped back before he could fasten his arms around her. "You're a good person, Jonathan. Happiness awaits you...go find it with someone else who will be happy with you. Let me move on with my own life."

"You're a lovely woman, Kierra. You deserve the best, even if it's without me."

"Bye," she said, confident in the permanence of this final separation.

"Take care." He squeezed her hand. "I promise not to disturb you again like I did the other day with the flowers." He grinned. "Do I get an A+ for making a fool of myself?"

"The other day," she echoed. She looked into his eyes. "Jonathan, did you call me this morning?"

"Call?" His voice had bumped up a notch in surprise. "No. I just crawled out of bed minutes before you arrived."

"Then, you're no fool." She hurried back to the car without a glance over her shoulder.

Kierra drove around the corner then veered to the curbside in need of calming her racing thoughts before continuing on. She sensed that things would remain good between them, and that Jonathan was sincere in wanting to leave her alone. But, that awful caller this morning. Who was he? She'd checked the caller ID, but the number went in one eye and out the other without registering in her exhausted brain. When she arrived back at the inn she'd look again to see if she recognized it, though the use of a public phone was a possibility. She ran a hand through her hair, her fingers twisting in the strands as if caught in a spider's web, and then remembered the text she'd received before she left Jonathan's. She whipped out her phone, hoping to find no news of an emergency.

Don't be angry with me, but Ryan's gone.

This from her mom? Ryan's gone...as in for the day or had he checked out? And why should she be angry with her mother?

a one-sentence note from Ryan, stuffed in an envelope with a surprise check for the remainder of the weeks he'd hoped to stay at the inn, greeted Kierra.

I have urgent matters to take care of.

Eight words, nine if she included his signature. No request to hold the room for his return. No forwarding address.

Sunshine streamed through the two narrow windows at the sides of the front door and spotlighted Anna's crinkled brow.

"Mom, what did Ryan say?"

"It's what I've said that you might want to know first." She pulled at her shirt collar. "Let's sit down."

This couldn't be good.

"Where are the troops?" Kierra asked, wanting to ascertain their privacy.

"Tessa and Zoe are enjoying a walk."

"Together?"

Anna nodded. "I know—isn't it wonderful? Since moving here, your sister is trying extra hard to re-bond with Zoe. And it's working." She latched onto Kierra's arm. "Want to settle in the kitchen for a cup of coffee?"

She needed fresh air, and to skip the caffeine. "How about out front? I certainly don't have guests about to check in."

"Hon, God's steps are miles ahead of you. He has your back. Your business will bloom again."

Kierra wanted badly to believe that everything in her life would bloom again. Spring shined around her, with summer around the corner. Yet, she didn't feel her heart opening and flourishing like it had the first day when Ryan had biked up the inn's driveway to check in. The past few days she'd dared to imagine if he might check into her life on a permanent basis. They could become a couple, an *us...we*. A husband and wife. But, now?

She looked at her mom. Their mother-daughter relationship had blossomed too, an unexpected blessing. If that could happen, what else waited in her near future?

"Let's go." Anna led the way outdoors. In the veranda they settled onto two neighboring Adirondack chairs. A catbird yowled in a nearby tree. "It's serene here."

Kierra nodded. The front view with its patch of woods across the road came close to rivaling the sight of Kindred Lake behind the inn. Yet, despite her mom's gentle reminder of how God always works on her behalf, peace remained aloof. She knew it shouldn't, but the human she was tilted toward the unhinged side. Wasn't that why she needed Him in her daily life more than ever?

God, please help me.

Kierra swiped her soggy palms on her legs, aware of her mom's observation of her every move. "Tell me what you said to Ryan. Did you ask him to leave?"

"Honey, I wouldn't do that."

Her mom never minced words. "You're right. You wouldn't have pushed him away. Sorry I doubted you. I was at Jonathan's and..." A look of shock flashed across Anna's face and stopped Kierra. She smiled softly. "The prank caller this morning left me riled. Thinking it was Jonathan I charged over to confront him, but I now know he wasn't the one."

A flicker of seconds ticked by. "You never told us about what was said during the call."

"The caller threatened to torch Kindred Lake Inn if I didn't keep out of his way."

Anna sprang to her feet and wrapped her arms around her middle. "And you went to Jonathan's rather than call the police?"

She tugged her mom back to her seat. "With the caller sounding a lot like Jonathan, I flew over there with the belief I could end this nonsense."

"But, we could be..." Anna swallowed visibly hard. "In jeopardy."

"Hear me out, Mom." She massaged a knot on her neck. "I confronted Jonathan about a few things that should have been said between us a while back and I have all the reason to believe he wasn't behind the call this morning. I can fill you in on the details later, but first let's talk about this text of yours I received while at Jonathan's. You said I shouldn't be angry with *you*, but that Ryan's gone. I'm confused. I can't imagine you sending him away unless he acted totally unscrupulous."

"No, he behaved like the perfect gentleman he is."

"Then why would I be upset with you?"

"After you and I talked last night and you'd retired to your room I stumbled across Ryan in the library. We had a nice chat." Anna looked downward to her lap. "You know, darling, he's kind of like the son I never had."

Kierra didn't like that her mom averted her gaze from her. "And?"

"I advised him to pay attention to his priorities and his heart. If he were to do both, he couldn't go wrong. After you left this morning, he packed his duffle, handed me the envelope, thanked me for the talk we had last night, and took off." Slowly, Anna met Kierra's eyes. "You're upset and I apologize. I should have never talked with him."

Kierra read Ryan's note again to see if she'd failed to detect a hidden meaning, but the message was simply stated with its emphasis that he needed to tend to matters.

In a short few weeks, vacationers would flock to the lake to enjoy picnics, boating, and hikes on its grassy shore. As if waking from a Brigadoon-sleep, the town would transform once more into a haven for many.

Kindred Lake, the town where love blossoms.

Love between family members.

Love between a man and a woman.

The love she and her mom and sister and niece had nurtured the past few weeks was as tangible as touching a silky blossom of a magnolia trees and becoming enlivened by its sweet candy scent.

For love to blossom between two it needed to be attended to with plenty of nourishment, warmth, and sunlight. Both recipients must treasure and respect the other, must grow strong together.

She faced her mother. "I've thought about lots since you and Tessa moved in. I want you to live permanently with me. There's certainly enough room and…" She trailed off when tears trickled down Anna's cheeks. "Oh, no." She covered her mouth with her hand. "My news is upsetting you."

"Kierra, sweetheart." Anna withdrew a tissue from a pant pocket and swiped at the tears. "You're making me happy, that's what you're doing. But we shouldn't interfere with your operation of running the inn or your personal life."

"Mom, my family is my priority. I love you…" She paused as Anna withdrew another tissue and blotted Kierra's runaway tears. "I will find it easier to make the inn work knowing you, Tessa, and Zoe are back in my life."

Anna sniffled and nodded. "What about Ryan? And what I said to him?"

"You spoke good, encouraging words to Ryan. I'm not upset with you. He knows where I am if he wants to contact me. I'm trusting God that whether Ryan comes back or not, that everything will work out fine for both of us."

"What about this threatening call? Should you phone the police?"

Kierra stood. "Yes. A threat shouldn't be taken lightly. I probably should have called them first before heading over to speak with Jonathan." A glance at her watch prompted her into action. "Pardon me, but I have a business to run and people to watch over. No time to lament over what I did or didn't do. I'll call the detective and see what he has to say."

The amplified bass on the rock station Bella had selected arrowed through Ryan's temples. He reached over and dialed off the car stereo.

"Hey, I like that song," Bella said in full out teen attitude.

"Trying to avoid a headache. Don't take it personally."

"What do we do until we get to your friends?"

Ryan let loose a soft chuckle. "Let's have an old-fashioned conversation."

"Like with each other?"

"Give me credit, kiddo. I'm always ready for good talk."

She arched a brow. "But Dad, you clammed when..." She slouched lower in the seat, likely wishing she could disappear.

"Bella, you're right. I had stopped talking professionally for a while, but it's time for me to put that behind."

She peeked at him then faced the road before them. "Whatcha going to do?"

"Honestly, a lot of that depends on you, sweetheart. As I've said, I'm putting you first in my life."

"But I don't want to get between you and anyone or anything else, like Kierra or you going back to reporting the news."

"Bella, if you didn't have to worry about me, your mom, or any one thing, where would you like to live?"

"With you," she said with no delay.

Both warmth and chills swirled within his chest. The last thing he expected for his daughter to say was that she wanted to live with him, a true honor and gift from God. He didn't want to ever disappoint her again.

She straightened in her seat, energy radiating from her. "Does this mean that I get to live with you and not move to Colorado with Mom? Are you going back to Baltimore or can you move to Kindred Lake? Are you going to marry Kierra...that would be cool and—"

"Hold on, there. It sounds like you want to live right where you are."

"Exactly. The school is cool, even better now that Zoe attends. I finally have a real friend with her. Her family is the greatest. You like them too, and you also like the town."

"Sounds like you're saying you've made roots."

"Kind of. But I can make deeper ones if I stay here instead of moving to a place where I don't know anyone." She lowered her chin. "It would be weird for you to visit me in Colorado, like what, like once or twice a year or for me show up at wherever you live. It's like I'll be a part-time daughter, just when I thought things were changing."

Ryan selfishly thought the same way, but he didn't want to separate Bella from her mother. "What about Mom? I think it would be best to have a woman in your life."

"Dad, get real. Mom's about to get hitched. She's starting a new life. She wants her privacy, and I don't want to be a pothole in the road to her happiness."

"A mom should always make room for her child."

She flashed him a classic stink eye. "What about a dad?"

She had him there. "You're right. Divorce is rotten, but it happens. I get it."

"That's what I want. How about you, Dad?"

He snaked his hand toward hers and gave it a squeeze. "I want you in my life. I want to be in your life. And, on a full-time basis."

"Then why are we going to your friends?"

"Like you with Zoe, I can benefit from a little talk with my pal. You'll like Zander and his wife, Jacey. Their little boy, Caleb, is adorable."

She settled back into the seat. "If you say so, it's all cool."

*C*aleb flung the front door open of the once small guest cabin, the one where his parents first met two winters ago. A huge smile stretched his lips, one that might have rivaled his fellow classmates discovering a puppy under a Christmas tree. Samson, their black-and-white Border collie, loped out the door and jumped around Ryan and Bella's legs.

Ryan snagged the dog's collar. "We love you too, Samson."

"Hi, Ryan." Caleb held up six fingers. "My birthday is in two days and I'll be six. Know what Mama and Daddy are getting me?"

"Hi, buddy." Ryan placed a hand on Bella's shoulder. "This is my daughter, Bella. And I haven't a clue as to what you're getting for your birthday."

"A baby brother or sister." Caleb bounced on his toes. He pointed at his red T-shirt with its Capital C. "I'm gonna be a big brother."

The little boy's enthusiasm hopped onto Ryan and he became bouncy with excitement. "Wow. Awesome news, my friend." He glanced over the boy's shoulder. "Where are Mom and Dad?"

"I'll get them." Caleb barely turned around when Jacey, followed by Zander, hurried down the hallway toward the door.

"Welcome," Jacey said, her arms opening for hugs. "Wow, you must be Bella. You look just like—"

"Like my Dad? I hear this lots." Bella grinned. "The kids at school think he looks hot. Me? Well, he's just Dad."

Zander laughed as he grabbed Ryan's hand and pulled him indoors. "Yes, Bella. Your old man's a looker...some guys have it made."

Jacey slipped an arm around her husband. "Oh, stop short-changing yourself. You're wonderful and I married you for a reason."

Zander scrunched his face. "Wait. I thought you said I-do because of my cooking skills."

"Well, that too." Jacey motioned for Ryan and Bella to have a seat. "Guess Caleb told you the big news that will happen in seven months." She sighed slowly. "Seven long, long months."

Zander squeezed her shoulders. "The time will fly fast enough."

"Congratulations," Ryan said. "I'm thrilled for you both. How are you feeling, Jacey?"

She rubbed her flat belly. "Mornings and late evenings are a bit rough, but I'm keeping my eyes on the blessed reward." She glanced at her son. "The doctor just confirmed my own suspicions this morning. Caleb is the first to know. Please excuse his energy level."

"I'm loving it." And Ryan did. Zander deserved this new beginning in life. He'd come close to losing his life when he was injured on the job three years ago. If it weren't for God's hand uniting him and Jacey in the middle of a blizzard, the direction his pal would have headed that day, and in life, might have been totally different. He had a new career in the state realty department, a beautiful home they'd expanded from its once little cabin size, and a baby of his own on the way. Aware of Jacey and Kierra's friendship, he couldn't wait to share the news with Kierra. He visualized her reaction: bright, smiling eyes, uttering a little squeal, and a congratulatory phone call with the arrangement of the two of them getting together for lunch and lots of talk and planning.

He held back a sigh.

Kierra.

He'd messed up, big time.

"Ryan?"

It wasn't until Ryan lifted his gaze had it occurred to him that he'd fixed his attention on the toes of his shoes.

"It's time for Samson's walk. Want to take a hike through the woods?" Zander widened his eyes at his wife.

"Bella," Jacey said. "How are you at making a tossed salad? I'm grilling ham and cheese for lunch. It's Caleb's favorite. The salad will go nicely. Let's stick around and let your dad and Zander take a walk."

Bella shrugged. "I'm so-so in the kitchen department, but I'll stick around."

"Mama," Caleb called. "Can I go on the walk too?"

Jacey made a funny face. "What did we talk about before Ryan and Bella got here?"

"About me coloring baby news?"

"That's right. The announcements to our family and friends about our baby need the special touch that only a big brother can offer. Get your crayons then meet us in the kitchen."

With Caleb happy to stay put with his mom and Bella, Ryan followed his good friend outdoors.

Zander pointed toward the hill behind the former guest cabin that they had transformed into a lovely log house with two extra bedrooms, and a larger eat-in kitchen. "I'll show you where we found Caleb pinned under the log during the blizzard."

"I've been wanting to see that site ever since you told me about it and how you, despite your injuries succeeded to pry it off of Caleb." Ryan narrowed his eyes at his pal. "You coping all right?"

"About the pain? Yeah, pretty good. Actually, if I keep up my daily walks, and move around a lot otherwise, I'm managing quite well, considering the pain is chronic." Zander chuckled. "Between work, a non-stop-until-bedtime son, and another child on the way, believe me, it's a rare day when I get to relax. But, I have to level with you, there's no other way I'd have it."

They kept silent until they reached the grassy hilltop. Samson happily greeted them with a woof clearly expressing his amazement about what took them so long. He then sped toward a fallen moss-covered log.

Ryan squinted against the sunlight. "Is that the infamous log?"

"That's the one. Caleb knows not to mess with it again, but we plan on removing it anyway especially with a baby on the way."

As they trudged across the swamp grass, Zander apologized for Ryan's shoes growing wet by the second. "There's a creek that funnels down from the upper hill. You wouldn't think its reach would make it this distance, but it does."

"Not a problem."

Zander hoisted one leg onto the log. "Then what is?"

"Pardon?"

"Ryan, it's me, Z. You can't hold back and think you're fooling me with that everything-is-awesome smile of yours."

Not concerned about the moisture, Ryan perched on the mossy log. "My multi-thousand dollar smile fooled my viewers for years."

"Well, I'm not one of them...and you, my friend, aren't presently on the air." Zander pursed his lips. "I'm thinking work isn't your chief problem, at least not what brought you for a visit today."

His pal was right. His once *contracted* and award-winning smile had successfully pulled in top ratings for his news team and the station, but that position no longer factored into the picture. And that was his choice.

On that first day when he biked into Kindred Lake with its

charming downtown, its scenic lake and hills, and its most attractive inn hostess, Kierra, his head spun in a 360 direction. No longer could he convince himself that the nightmare of the fires, of the tragic loss of life he'd witnessed, prevented him from returning.

He wanted out of that former lifestyle. But how?

Zander placed a hand on Ryan's shoulder. "I was Best Man at your wedding and the first of friends to see Bella when she was born. You took me out to the swankiest of Maryland's restaurants when I made Detective. I let you camp out in my spare bedroom when you split with Lisa. You, my pal, sat beside my hospital bed and prayed over me then did the same when I went into rehab. We've been through a lot together. So don't think for a second that I'm about to leave your side."

Ryan, with emotion pressing down on his tongue, slumped forward and rested his elbows on his knees. "I thought I couldn't return to broadcasting the news." He gulped down the difficulty of his confession he needed to tell. "I blamed it on those cursed fires, on losing that child. Since then, I've come to see a whole different slice of life in Kindred Lake. I realize I don't miss the old ways."

Zander sat beside him. "Who is it?"

"Who? It's what. It's Kindred Lake, the town."

"It's never a place, buddy. It's always a person your soul leaps for."

Ryan sat up. "You're right. It's my daughter. I want to continue being an active dad in her life, not someone she sees once or twice a year."

Zander shook his head, but smiled. "I love your devotion to your kid. That's the way it should be between a father and his children and believe me, you're hero material in my eyes."

"Oh, please."

"If you don't like that term, then settle for role model. I want to be the best dad ever for my kids and I admire how you're there for others and how you cling to your faith in God. But something —and I'm thinking it's you—is preventing you from going after the beauty of life, in this case, a woman."

"You're right." Slowly, he faced his friend. "Her name is Kierra."

"Ah, Jacey's friend. And you're in love with her?"

"Yes." The reply came without hesitation. "Yes," he repeated, louder.

"Awesome news, buddy. You love Kierra, and I'm believing she loves you because what's not to love about you?"

Ryan opened his mouth, but Zander held up his hands.

"Hold on, there. Think what the Bible says about love: how it's patient, kind, trusts, hopes, and perseveres. If all these exists between you two, what's holding you back?"

"Actually, nothing. You may be right."

"I'll utter my *of course I am* later."

"Good." Ryan smirked. "Reporting the news taught me to always expect the unexpected in life. Kindred Lake has taught me that relationships are fragile and must be treasured. I think I caught this floundering fatherhood thing with Bella in time to patch things up better than ever, but as for Kierra, I fear it's too late between us."

"It's never late for love. Nor is it ever too late to let go of fear. Fear's the culprit keeping you from enjoying a happy forever and ever."

"How?"

Zander waved his hand. "Look at this place and imagine it covered deep in snow."

"Like the time you and Jacey were searching for Caleb?"

Zander nodded. "Jacey was afraid of not finding Caleb before harm came his way."

"Understandable. How did you comfort her?"

"I'll ask you the same question I asked her."

"Shoot."

"Do you believe in God, Ryan?"

"You bet."

"Then show me."

"I don't understand."

Zander smiled softly. "Those were Jacey's exact words. And I'll respond to you in the same way. Show me how you cling to the God you believe won't fail you."

Ryan stood. Samson padded over, his tail wagging, imploring with his eyes for a pat. Ryan obliged.

"You're a good friend, Z. I hope Jacey doesn't mind if Bella and I cut out before lunch, but it's best if we leave."

"And why is that?"

"There's a certain woman I left back in Kindred Lake, a special, wonderful person I need to reassure that with God on our sides, always watching our comings and goings, that we can step into the future, together."

Zander gave a thumbs up. "I was counting on you saying that."

At the inn's front door, Kierra smiled at the sights of luscious mid-May spring and breathed in deep its sweet scents. Trees leafed out in bright green; the rhododendron splashed blue, pink, and yellow; dogwoods added their royal white. Trumpet-shaped honeysuckle flowers, with its intoxicating aroma, was enough to keep her glued to her front yard for hours if she didn't have to work. Spring, the season of rebirth, was truly a glimpse of heaven on earth.

Kierra swallowed hard and did a double take. Oh, boy. HoJo, driving his patrol car with Zoe in the front seat, crested the driveway. More amazing was the sight of Ryan pedaling his bike right behind. She leaned against the doorjamb to steady her wobbly self.

Zoe jumped out of the car, her wrists free from handcuffs. A good sign.

"Aunt Kierra, wait until you hear what happened."

Before Kierra could respond, the door behind her creaked further open. Tessa hurled herself at her daughter and enveloped her into an embrace. A gentle pat on Kierra's shoulder swung her around to see her mom standing behind her. Anna's lifted brow indicated she was also clueless to what was happening.

"I didn't know Zoe wasn't around," Kierra said in confession to her mother.

"Me neither."

They hurried over.

"Zoe, what's happening, baby?" Tessa said. "I just got your text that you're in a police car." She pulled back from Zoe and covered her heart. "You scared me awful."

"Sorry, Mom. But I couldn't take this droopiness crawling around this place a minute longer. It was like living in a dungeon without windows showing life outside. I had to do this, even if it meant doing it myself since Bella wasn't around." Zoe wrapped her arms around her middle. "I miss her."

"We've all missed Bella." Tessa glanced at Ryan. "And you as well."

Tessa's concerned look kicked Kierra into gear. "HoJo, what's happening? Officer Ben isn't with you?"

"He is presently booking the suspects we just picked up thanks to your niece."

Tessa again swung an arm around her daughter. "Details from the beginning, please, before my nerves disintegrate."

HoJo and Zoe exchanged looks.

"Why don't you tell your family about what happened?" the detective said.

"I guess you're right," Zoe said. Her attention flitted to the others then settled back on Tessa. "But Mom, don't go bonkers. Let me tell the full story."

"Go ahead," Tessa replied, more softly this time.

"As I said," Zoe began, "I got fed up with everyone upset over the two weeks Ryan and Bella haven't visited, plus the fear of that stupid threat Aunt Kierra got"—she eyed Kierra, as if to say, *yeah, I know about that phone call*—"about burning down this place. And Bella wasn't answering my texts, at least not until this morning when she replied saying all's finally okay, whatever that meant."

Both Zoe and Kierra looked at Ryan.

"One thing at a time, don't you think?" he said, gentleness lacing his tone.

"Yeah, you're probably right." Zoe paused for a few seconds, her girlish, nervous tone betraying her exterior toughness. "You guys are my only family and I love you. You mean everything to me. Ryan, I mean that too about you and Bella. Anyways, I kept going over and over in my head about who could be lame enough to start fires in this little town, and who would dare mess with Aunt Kierra and her inn. Last night I went to see that stupid drug pusher where you found me and Bella in his car."

Tessa gasped.

"But I swear, Mom, I didn't go to get drugs. Do you believe me?"

"Of course I do."

Zoe sighed her relief. "I pumped the creep for information, told him I'd rat him out to the cops about his hidden drug supply and network of pushers if he didn't confess and—"

"Oh, Zoe. You might have been hurt...might have been..." Tessa trailed off, swiping her eyes and sniffling.

"Well, I wasn't."

"We'll talk more about this later, but you must never again take things like this into your own hands," Tessa said in a soft, but firm tone. "Please continue."

"He said he and his older cousin started a couple of fires around town because they were bored. Then Cuz wanted to make more trouble. They got talking about me, and knew where I was living. They schemed this degenerate prank on Aunt Kierra with that phone call." Her glanced at Ryan. "That's the day when Ryan left."

"The two suspects that Zoe speaks about have confessed," HoJo said. He turned toward Zoe. "Anything else?"

Zoe smirked. "Just that I called the police this morning and ratted them out, anyways. Since I phoned from the downtown diner, Officer HoJo got me and brought me to the station to wait while he went after them."

"They're both under arrest for drugs, harassment, and likely arson," HoJo said. He faced Zoe. "If I were you, I'd follow your mom's advice and never confront a possible suspect again, whether alone or with another individual."

"Sounds cool," Zoe said.

Out of the corner of her eye, Kierra saw her sister mouth a thank-you to the officer.

"I'm needed back at the precinct." HoJo handed business cards to Kierra, Tessa, and Ryan with the instruction to phone with any other questions. He wished them a good day and took off.

Tessa patted Zoe's shoulder. "Why don't we go indoors and have ourselves a little discussion?"

"Oh, Mom..."

With her arm around Zoe, Tessa led her toward the inn.

"Wait," Anna called. "Is there room for me?"

Tessa turned around. "Always, Mom." The three continued indoors.

Kierra remembered the mantra she created upon their moving-in day. *Family first.* Always. Praise God for how He blessed her family and reunited them.

"May we talk?" Ryan said.

Kierra glanced at her watch. "Cami and Gavin are about to arrive to discuss final wedding details." As if on cue, a blue Honda sped up the driveway. "And there they are."

"Wow," Cami called out the second she stepped out of the car. "Have I news for you, and it's not the greatest."

"Mind if I stay?" Ryan murmured as Cami approached.

Kierra's heart pounded. The ache. The joy. The confusion. "I guess that's fine."

Cami caught up with them. "Brodie Sullivan, my fiddler, canceled for the ceremony. What are we supposed to do?"

Kierra smiled in hope of reassurance. "That's unfortunate, but I have a file of other musicians I'll show you and you'll likely find a group to your liking." She grasped her friend's hand and greeted Gavin beside his bride-to-be. Kierra introduced Ryan to them both and asked if they minded whether he joined them.

Cami flashed Ryan a huge smile. "Nice to meet you, Ryan. Are you looking to gain insight to planning a wedding?"

"It's a possibility," Ryan said.

Kierra didn't know how to interpret his serious expression. Had he a girlfriend that he hadn't informed her about? Was that why he'd taken off?

Ryan looked at Cami and Gavin. "Do you mind if I borrow Kierra for a few minutes?"

"We're in no rush." Gavin put an arm around his wife-to-be. "Cami and I are spending eternity together. Take all the time you need."

Ryan thanked them then smiled at Kierra. "Let's go down to the lake."

Determined to stick with business, a safe topic, she planned to ask him if he'd like to continue to rent his room. On the way to the lake they passed the gazebo where Cami and Gavin would soon affirm their love in the form of wedding vows...the gazebo where she'd heard Ryan tell his daughter basically it was over between them.

Enough, she ordered herself. Focus on the now, not what happened, what could have happened.

At the lakeside Ryan encircled her in his arms. At first she stiffened, but when he kissed her, and didn't stop, she was unable to deny she wanted him. She leaned in for more. This must be love, not just hungry desire. She wanted his sweet affection and tenderness, his love. His presence and warmth swept her away to things wonderful. Rainbow skies. Songbirds'calls. The heady smell of spring blossoms.

He pulled back first. She didn't want him to.

"I've thought about a lot these past few weeks," he said. "I'm moving to Kindred Lake, this special town of enchantment, slow-paced living, and you."

And you.

Her heart pounded, yet peace seeped throughout her. Was that physically possible?

"Is your daughter cool about this? What about your job with the station?"

"Bella is ecstatic. I've started the process of obtaining full-time custody of her, which her mom isn't contesting. Plus, she has come to love and admire you, as well as your family." He studied her. "You are beaming."

"That's because I'm loving how this is turning out for both of us. I've asked my family to stay permanently at the inn with me. Tessa has a job interview lined up for tomorrow and Mom's running with your suggestion of starting a second blog for parents. We need to work out the details about living space. That apartment where I live in the carriage house can easily be converted to a full size home...there are lots of possibilities."

"If that was my mom, sister and niece I'd do the same."

She jumped in joy, her spirit truly lifted. "I'm thrilled for you two. Bella will love it here knowing she can come home to you."

"As well as have you and your family as part of her life."

"Absolutely, Ryan. I don't want it any other way."

"As for the news anchor position, it's past tense. I have an interview lined up tomorrow at a Philly newspaper to work in their editorial department, one that I could do from home on the days I choose not to commute. It sounds promising."

"Where would you stay?"

"I plan to start house hunting tomorrow."

"I have a confession to make." She wasn't about to stop when he lifted a questioning brow. "I've grown fond of you. Extremely."

He pulled her back into his embrace. "Have you?"

"We make quite the team together. A perfect fit."

"Yes, we do. A comfortable one."

She was going to spill it all before him. "If the job offer doesn't come through I'd love for you to consider partnering with me running the inn because...well...operating this place by myself is a lot of work for one person."

He lifted her and swung her around, his strength a balm of stability, certainty, and most definitely happiness. "I'd love that."

"There's enough room at the inn for you and Bella to live as well."

He released her down to the ground. "Is that room as in a guestroom or room in your heart because I want to partner with you more than on the business level?"

"In my heart," she murmured, her vision blurry from the happy tears of finding the true love God meant for her. "Always."

"I love you, Kierra. I want you in my life for always." From his shirt pocket he withdrew a diamond ring and slipped it onto her left ring finger. "Will you marry me?"

"Yes." She pulled him into an embrace, the place she longed to be, for always. Looking deep into her future husband's beautiful eyes, with the background of Kindred Lake, she heard the music of blessings to come, ones with Ryan and Bella, and her reunited family.

ACKNOWLEDGMENTS

A big thanks to my Avenue E Street Team. Writing and publishing can be overwhelming at times and I'm blessed by your support.

To my sweet friend, Roberta C.M. DeCaprio, who wanted to see more of The Lemonade Girls. I'm thankful for your encouragement—about everything!—through the years.

And once again, to my friends, authors Megan Whitson Lee and Kathleen Rouser, and eye-sharp readers Kay Moorehouse and Paula Marie, for your support and editorial comments.

Elaine Stock is an award-winning author of Women's & Inspirational Fiction to uplift with hope of better tomorrows. Her novel, *Her Good Girl*, received the Outstanding Christian/Religious Fiction Award in the 2018 IAN Book of the Year Awards, 2018 Readers' Favorite Silver Medal in Christian Fiction and the 2018 American Fiction Awards in the Christian Inspirational category.

Elaine is a member of Women's Fiction Writers Association, American Christian Fiction Writers, and the Romance Writers of America. Born in Brooklyn, NY, Elaine has now been living in upstate, rural New York with her husband for more years than her stint as a NYC gal. She enjoys long walks down country roads, visiting New England towns, and of course, a good book.

Please visit Elaine at: https://elainestock.com

Thank you for reading *When Love Blossoms*. Please consider leaving a review on Amazon, Goodreads, and BookBub. I would be most grateful. A review truly helps an author.

Connect With Elaine on:

facebook.com/AuthorElaineStock

twitter.com/ElaineStock

goodreads.com/ElaineStock

bookbub.com/authors/elaine-stock

ALSO BY ELAINE STOCK

Always With You: Winner of the 2017 Christian Small Publisher Book of the Year Award in fiction, a tale of falling in love with a man you were warned to stay away from.

Amazon: http://amzn.to/2IuGtGF

Barnes and Noble: http://bit.ly/1PfRyXX

Her Good Girl: 3x award winner in Christian inspirational fiction, the story of what happens to a family when the hurt gets so bad that an outsider decides to take things into his own hands and it may not be for the better.

Amazon: http://amzn.to/2loWMxM

Christmas Love Year Round: Book 1 of the Kindred Lake Series

Amazon: https://amzn.to/2wnp2z8

Look for Book 3 of the Kindred Lake Series, *The Colors of Love*